NEVER A TRAITOR

BOOK COLLECTIONS BY JAN THOMPSON

Protector Sweethearts (6 Books)

JanThompson.com/protector

Defender Sweethearts (6 Books)

JanThompson.com/defender

Binary Hackers (3 Books)

JanThompson.com/binary

Seaside Chapel (12 Books)

JanThompson.com/seaside

Savannah Sweethearts (13 Books)

JanThompson.com/savannah

Vacation Sweethearts (8 Books)

JanThompson.com/vacation

Sign up for Jan's mailing list to be notified when new books are published:

JanThompson.com/newsletter

NEVER A TRAITOR

DEFENDER SWEETHEARTS BOOK 1

JAN THOMPSON

GEORGIA
PRESS

Never a Traitor (Defender Sweethearts Book 1)

Copyright © 2020 Jan Edttii Lim Thompson

Author Website: JanThompson.com
Book News: JanThompson.com/newsletter

Published by Georgia Press LLC

This book is a work of fiction. All characters, persons, places, events, and things either are the product of the author's active imagination or are used fictitiously.

Scripture taken from the New King James Version®. Copyright © 1982 by Thomas Nelson. Used by permission. All rights reserved.

Cover Design: Indie Cover Design

eBook ISBN: 978-1-944188-67-2
Paperback ISBN: 978-1-944188-69-6

To my Lord and Savior, Jesus Christ, who died on the cross to save me from my sins and rose again from the grave to give me eternal life in heaven.

For God so loved the world that He gave His only begotten Son, that whoever believes in Him should not perish but have everlasting life.
—John 3:16

READ A FREE EBOOK IN THE SAME STORY WORLD

Set in Georgia, South Carolina, and Tennessee, this clean and wholesome Christian romance tells the story of art gallery archivist Sheryl Breckenridge and world-famous sculptor Winton Pace. Read this ebook for free!

Time for Me (A Vacation Sweethearts Prequel)
JanThompson.com/time-free

ABOUT DEFENDER SWEETHEARTS
CHRISTIAN ROMANTIC SUSPENSE NOVELS

Defender Sweethearts is a sister series to the Protector Sweethearts Christian romantic suspense collection. While the heroes in Protector Sweethearts search for lost treasures and lost people, the Defender Sweethearts novels focus on protecting the helpless and hopeless.

- Book 1: *Never a Traitor*
- Book 2: *Never a Hostage*
- Book 3: *Never a Fugitive*
- Book 4: *Always a Maverick*
- Book 5: *Always a Champion*
- Book 6: *Always a Guardian*

For more information about Defender Sweethearts:
JanThompson.com/defender

ABOUT NEVER A TRAITOR
DEFENDER SWEETHEARTS BOOK 1

A paranoid whistleblower on her last task. A private investigator posing as her fake boyfriend. An international conglomerate that eliminates its enemies.

Calling for help...

Administrative Assistant Sienna Halstead has one last task to do for the FBI Criminal Investigative Division before she can quit her corporate job and disappear. Scared that the evidence against the international conglomerate she works for is not sufficient, paranoid Sienna starts to make mistakes. When she calls Hu Knows, Inc., for help, Helen Hu sends the no-nonsense Earl into her chaotic world.

Cashing in on overtime pay...

The last thing Private Investigator Earl Young expects to do on his week off is to pose as a fake boyfriend to one of two whistleblowers at a business convention, although the former Special Ops soldier is confident he can handle any task his employer assigns to him. Besides, he gets to stay at a five-star hotel and eat for free.

Crossing the line...

Earl's driving need to solve problems forces him to work alongside Sienna as she draws him deeper into her corporate world of secrets and subterfuge.

The more time they spend time together, the more Earl feels attracted to Sienna, and forgets that he is only her bodyguard. When Sienna's life is endangered, how far will Earl go to protect her?

Never a Traitor is book 1 in *USA Today* bestselling author Jan Thompson's Defender Sweethearts Christian romantic suspense collection, a sister series to Protector Sweethearts. While the heroes in Protector Sweethearts search for lost treasures and lost people, the Defender Sweethearts novels focus on protecting the helpless and hopeless. The main characters in Defender Sweethearts come from the supporting cast in Protector Sweethearts.

Never a Traitor (Defender Sweethearts Book 1)
JanThompson.com/traitor

Defender Sweethearts
JanThompson.com/defender

For Book News from Jan Thompson:
JanThompson.com/newsletter

NEVER A TRAITOR

CHAPTER ONE

S ienna Halstead regretted letting Private Investigator Earl Young tag along with her to visit a former coworker. Earl's presence caused Dana Nesbitt to be extra nervous, and now Sienna couldn't get her to talk in detail about what she had overheard their CEO say, anything that could be useful to FBI investigations.

"I was only the accountant," Dana said, in between deep puffs of smoke. "He didn't have to fire me. I wouldn't have talked."

Sitting in a worn armchair across from the shabby couch, Sienna held her breath and prayed that her lungs would survive the conversation. Where was her mask when she needed it?

She could see the headlines now.

Administrative assistant died from smoke inhalation. Buried in an unmarked grave. Case unsolved.

Earl was fortunate, then. Sienna had sent him outside to wait in the great outdoors so that Dana could speak freely inside her own home.

Sienna felt bad that she had to lie to Dana about her relationship with Earl. No, he wasn't really her boyfriend, but the ruse was necessary to prevent Dana or Sienna or anyone else from getting killed. Technically, neither Sienna nor Earl had said they were an item. They simply let Dana put two and two together without correcting her.

Dissimulation was a form of lying, nonetheless.

Sienna closed her eyes. She wanted this entire project to be over as soon as possible so she could leave the company and disappear. She was no longer impressed by the size and scope of Gavard Owens Oppenheimer Properties or by the quiet and studious Finnegan Ford, the CEO and half brother of Zachary Gavard, the smooth-talking front man of GOOP.

Dana lit another cigarette and shrugged. "Why am I so worried? Everyone sleeps with him."

Sienna prayed for the right words to say. Mom's words came to mind.

When in doubt, speak the truth.

"I didn't," Sienna said.

"You're different." Dana laughed nervously. "You're religious. Finnegan is scared of you."

"He told you that?"

"I could tell. He would never touch you like he touched everyone else..." Dana started to cry. "I wish I never..."

"Oh, Dana." Sienna sprung up from her armchair to get to Dana, and heard a rip. She looked down to find her linen pants torn on one side, part of the fabric stuck at the end of a giant spring that had somehow shot out of the threadbare armchair. "Whoa."

She checked her thigh to see if there was a cut —and whether she needed a tetanus shot.

Thank God there was no cut.

She tugged her pants away from the spring, and hobbled around the chipped coffee table, her arms waving away the smoke until she found the petite and helpless Dana on the couch, weeping.

"Should I keep the baby?" Dana's voice was tinged with regret and anger and probably a million other emotions.

Sienna wondered how a pastor's kid such as Dana could turn out this way. Sienna prayed for the right words to say to her friend.

"Shhh." That was all that came out of her

mouth as she sat there, holding smoky Dana in her arms—

Wait a minute.

"You shouldn't smoke if you're carrying a baby." Okay, wrong words. She should be more diplomatic.

"Don't tell me what to do!" Dana pulled away from Sienna's arms.

Sienna blinked in the smoke, her eyes stinging. She was still partly holding her breath, and now she felt dizzy.

I have to get out of here.

However, she could not ask Dana to take a walk with her. It was too dangerous for Dana to be outdoors. In fact, she had to leave town and go somewhere safe.

"Can you get out of town for a few days until we figure out what's going on?" Sienna coughed. She had read somewhere that secondary smoke was really bad.

"Where do I go?"

"Somewhere nobody would find you." Sienna lifted the collar of her blouse over her nose.

Dana's eyebrows shot up. "You mean like Alaska or Hawaii? Or maybe the Amalfi Coast?"

"I was thinking someplace more affordable."

"Like where?"

"I don't know, but you can't stay here."

"Here is all I can afford." Dana jammed the rest of her cigarette in the tray, bending it out of shape. "He won't give me any more money."

"You asked him?" As in blackmail?

Dana barely nodded.

"Did you tell him about the child?" Sienna asked.

"Before I left the company."

"What did he say?"

"That's a perk for employees only." Dana made a face. "He was trying to rub it in. Told me in no uncertain terms that I shouldn't have quit."

It had been sudden. Even Sienna didn't know about it until the next day when she went to work and saw Dana's desk cleaned out. It took Sienna a week to find Dana hiding away in this rat hole.

She had to give Earl credit for tracking down Dana.

"I can't believe he moved on to Genevieve." Dana reached for her cigarettes.

Sienna pushed the lighter away. "Genevieve in the mailroom?"

"Is there another woman with repeated wardrobe malfunctions in front of every senior staffer?"

"Well..." Sienna prayed for mercy. She had

made up her mind that as soon as this final project was over, she would leave the company. It was a cesspool of sin, as Uncle Tabbebo had called GOOP. He wanted her to leave the company and put her college degree to better use.

However, the FBI Special Agent had told her that if she did this one thing for them, it would shut down GOOP forever. And they would put her in the Federal Witness Security Program, in which she would never have to worry about looking over her shoulder for the rest of her life.

Unfortunately, it also meant she would not see Mom and Uncle Tabbebo again. They would be devastated.

Unless she could take down GOOP anonymously.

Which was where Dana came in.

Sienna's only hope shook her head. "I should've known. Why didn't you tell me he was no good?"

"I did. Countless times."

"I guess I wasn't listening."

"No." Sienna wanted to ask Dana how Mr. Ford had seduced her, but this wasn't the right time.

Well, she didn't have to ask.

"I loved his offers. Nights in five-star hotels.

Private jets. Weekends on his yacht. Dining with his friends. I loved it all."

"What friends did he have dinner with?" Sienna asked.

"High rollers, investors, and in one case, even his brother showed up."

"You mean Mr. Gavard?" Bingo.

"I know, right? His brother never showed up at any of Finnegan's events. But that one time two months ago..." Dana straightened up. "He was staring at me the whole time. You know how we hate each other?"

"Yeah, even though you're his accountant too."

"Well, I don't do more than I have to." Dana sighed.

"You were saying that Mr. Gavard showed up on the yacht. Did he get into an argument with his brother?"

"It wasn't like that. Although it was strange that he disappeared with Finnegan into our stateroom for what seemed like hours."

"Stateroom?" Sienna asked. "So this was on his superyacht?"

"Actually, let me correct myself. They were in our suite. Finnegan had to remind me a lot that staterooms are smaller. Our suite took up the entire upper floor of the yacht."

"Wow."

"I know, right? I mean what do you expect? The yacht is worth a hundred million dollars."

"No way." Sienna couldn't imagine. "Must be souped up."

Dana nodded. "It even has a helipad. That's how Zachary flew in on a chopper. Can you believe it? Landed right on top of the yacht. That was how he left too. Didn't stay for dinner."

"What did they talk about?" Sienna asked.

Dana gave her a look. "I really like his wife."

"His wife?"

Why had Dana brought up Gavard's wife at all? Celestia Gavard had nothing to do with the day-to-day operations at her husband's company, as far as Sienna knew. She was a silent partner—she poured her inheritance money into it—but that was all.

Dana pursed her lips.

"So you do know more about what's happening than you're letting on," Sienna said.

"Probably why I got fired." Dana sniffled.

"You said the brothers talked privately." Sienna wondered if she should record this conversation, but this was Dana, her friend, who had gone through so much in the last two months that she deserved some privacy.

Perhaps Sienna could gain Dana's trust and then have her repeat whatever it was she was about to say.

Instead, Dana reached below her collar and pulled out her necklace. At the end of the necklace was a pendant that looked like a silver whistle. She took the necklace off and handed it to Sienna.

"What is this?" Sienna looked at the whistle.

"I'm giving it to you."

"Me?"

"Happy belated birthday, Sienna."

"That's thoughtful of you." Sienna had no idea what was swirling in Dana's head. She wondered if she could go around wearing a whistle on her neck.

"It's sterling silver. Sorry it's not gold."

"I don't care." Sienna put it around her own neck.

Dana expelled a breath. "That felt better."

"What felt better?"

"It was so heavy around my neck. Like a noose, you know?"

"This whistle?" Sienna asked.

Dana nodded. "Please keep it for me?"

"I thought it was a gift."

"Yes. It's yours now. But it's also my insurance."

"What are you talking about?" The last thing Sienna wanted was to be responsible for something that wasn't her own. "What is this? Does it even work?"

"It works."

And another last thing Sienna wanted was someone else's used whistle.

"I'll explain later." Dana touched her stomach. She got up, drew a deep breath. "I'm thirsty again. Do pregnant people get thirsty all the time?"

"I have no idea." Still staring at the whistle, Sienna had second thoughts about the gift.

Dana opened an old refrigerator in her studio kitchen. Behind her, a farmhouse sink backed up against a wall with a small window. Outside the window, there was a fence that seemed to be too close to the ramshackle house. The sun was setting and the fence looked dark and weary.

"Would you like some water?" Dana asked.

"Yes." But she almost said no, when she saw Dana pour unfiltered water from the sink faucet into a plastic cup she had picked up from the countertop.

Was that cup even washed?

Sienna was going to put the necklace into her crossbody bag when she realized she didn't have it with her. She must have left it in Earl's SUV, together with her phone and pepper spray inside.

She was about to put the necklace into the

pocket of her ripped pants when she heard shattering glass.

Her eyes snapped up just as Dana collapsed to the ground, the plastic cup bouncing off the old linoleum floor. The kitchen faucet was still running. The window above the sink looked broken.

"Dana!" Sienna gasped as the house went silent.

Sienna threw herself on the ugly green rug between the coffee table and the couch, and held her breath. She wished she had her phone with her.

She could not call Earl. Could not call 911.

The only Person she could call was God.

Help me, Jesus!

From the corner of her eye, she saw someone move in the hallway between the kitchen and the bedroom. She looked up to see the figure moving toward her, dressed in black from head to toe, with a ski mask and goggles.

Sienna froze when she saw the silencer pointed in her direction.

"Give it to me." It was a low male voice.

He sounded like he could hurt her.

"Give what?" Sienna bravely asked.

"What she gave to you."

"She was getting me water."

Ninja grunted. "You're not stupid."

"Thank you for the vote of confidence."

He inched closer. "Now."

"I don't know what you're—"

A blast blew Ninja back, his weapon flying out of his hand. He landed on the green carpet, blood seeping out of his ski mask. He went still.

Sienna screamed.

CHAPTER TWO

A strong hand touched Sienna's arm.

"It's me. Let's go." Calm, quiet voice. Deep, soothing voice.

Earl Young.

Sienna scrambled to her feet, holding on to his hand as he pulled her up. She reached down to grab her Mary Jane that had fallen off her foot. She put it back on, and reminded herself to wear boots the next time she made a house call, in case she needed to run to safety or something.

Around them, half a dozen heavily armed people swarmed the small living room, wearing helmets, protective armor, and vests that said "FBI."

Someone came up to them and talked to Earl.

Sienna could hardly recognize her in her protective armor and goggles. But as soon as she started speaking, Sienna knew that was FBI Special Agent Mariana Kimball.

"Once again, Sienna." Kimball smacked her lips to show her great disappointment. "Why are you doing this alone when you can have federal forces with you?"

"She wouldn't have talked," Sienna defended herself.

"Did she?" Kimball asked.

"Well, we were getting to it."

Kimball shook her head. "You need to leave now. You cannot be seen here."

"Thanks for coming, Agent Kimball," Earl said. "And please cut her some slack. She's losing her job, and she's losing her freedom."

Before Sienna could say anything, another agent approached them but he spoke directly to Kimball. "Ma'am, she's still breathing. Paramedics are on the way."

"Dana!" Sienna tried to get to her friend.

"Visit her at the hospital later. We need to get you to safety." Kimball pushed her back and strong-armed her through the crowd of other agents toward the front door. To Earl, she said, "Where's your vehicle?"

"Two houses down," Earl said.

"Give me the key and we'll move it for you." The agent waved to an unmarked van by the curb. "Go now. We'll talk soon."

"Wait," Sienna said to Earl. "I left my purse in your SUV."

"No, you didn't." Earl reached in between two shriveled-up bushes outside the front door, and retrieved her crossbody bag. It was covered with mud and dirt. "Sorry about that. I had no time to find a place for it. I heard the first shot and thought you were..."

Dead?

"It could've been very bad," Sienna said. "Thank you."

Agent Kimball opened the van door for them. "Earl, thanks. You got here a second before we did."

"A minute."

"Splitting hairs."

"Still, you owe me dinner." Earl chuckled.

"No, I don't. Get in." Kimball pointed to the backseat.

"Don't you want me to drive?" Earl remained standing by the van door.

"No, Earl. My guy will take you to the safe house." She waved for someone to come over. She handed him the key and told him where to take Earl and Sienna.

"Nice to have a chauffeur," Earl said.

Kimball ignored him. She looked Sienna up and down. "Next time you visit a witness, don't go alone. If you want to stay alive, never leave his side."

"I was nearby," Earl said as he helped Sienna into the van.

"Are you defending her?"

"Just telling you I rushed in as fast—and as safely—as I could." Earl got in and sat down next to Sienna. He turned to the agent. "Sorry about your guy in the car. I couldn't get to him in time."

"Can't be in two places at once," the agent said.

Or can you?

As Sienna listened to them, she recalled what Dana had said to her. In the yacht two months before, the two half brothers had a long conversation. Dana said she wasn't in the suite with them. But she seemed to indicate that she had an inkling of what they were discussing. How could she be in two places at the same time?

Sienna reached into her pocket. The necklace and whistle were still there. Would she need to turn them over to the FBI? When? Maybe after she figured out what the whistle was?

Then again, the FBI had more resources than she did.

Sienna knew she had to talk to Earl about the evidence she was now hiding—momentarily—from the FBI.

Agent Kimball left them to wait for an ambulance that pulled up in front of the house. In the surreal moment, Sienna hadn't heard the ambulance siren at all. Sienna watched the paramedics roll a stretcher into the house.

"I need to go to Dana." Sienna unbuckled her seat belt.

"No." Earl stopped her. "If we don't get out of here, Dana might not be the only one shot."

As the driver drove the FBI van away from the crime scene, Sienna realized her blouse smelled like cigarette smoke. She tried to fan it away.

Buckled in next to her on the bench seat at the back of the van, Earl turned to her. "Are you okay?"

"Do I smell like smoke?" Sienna asked.

"A little."

"I need a shower. Will they let me go home?"

"No. We need you alive. We'll be at the safe house until it's time to go to the airport."

Sienna's eyebrows rose. "If I can't go home, then my friend from church can't go to my house either, right?"

"No, but I paid someone to keep an eye on your house."

"Is he going to feed my cat?"

"You have a cat?" Earl looked like he had missed a major piece of information.

"Helen didn't tell you?"

"No." Earl grunted. "What's the cat's name?"

"Wyclef."

"Really."

"Yeah. So who's going to feed my cat?"

Earl sighed. He called someone on his phone and told him what Sienna had asked.

"You just have to, okay? Yeah, man. I'll let you talk to her," he said, then handed the phone to Sienna. "Tell him where the cat food is."

"Hello?" Sienna said into the phone, telling Earl's guy where the pantry was and how often the water bowl needed to be changed. "Why don't you just stay in the house instead of coming and going? You can sleep in the guest bedroom. Yes, eat whatever you want. I'll be home this coming weekend."

When she hung up, Earl stared at her. "You invited a stranger to live in your house."

"You trusted him. Helen trusted you. It will all work out."

"Otherwise you'll sue us." Earl chuckled.

The van driver also chuckled. "Don't sue me. I got nothing to do with your cat."

Sienna breathed a sigh of relief now that her cat was going to be taken care of. "Do you have pets, Earl?"

"Nope."

"Well. They do take effort and energy."

"I'm too busy," Earl said. "No time."

"Speaking of time, God sent you just in time," Sienna said before she remembered to self-correct what she said to people at work and in general.

Many times, nobody in her secular world wanted to hear talk about God. They would tell her to keep her *religion* to herself. It wasn't a religion as much as a relationship with God through Jesus Christ, but Sienna was tired of explaining.

Now, in the trenches, her true self had emerged. She had called out to God back there in that house after Dana was shot, and God had answered her prayer.

I'm alive. Dana's alive.

"Glad you believe in God," Earl said quietly.

"Do you?"

"There are more people in this world who do than you can see." Earl pointed to the torn fabric of Sienna's pants. "Are you hurt?"

19

"Ah, no," Sienna covered her exposed thigh with a palm. "Battle with the armchair."

"A spring sprung?" Earl chuckled.

"My friend has been shot, and you're laughing?" Sienna snapped.

"I'm not. Trust me. I'm a serious guy."

"I led them to her." Sienna blinked.

"We don't know that." Earl's eyes met hers.

It was twilight outside, and Sienna couldn't remember the color of Earl's eyes. They were dark now, and still staring at her. They were kind eyes, but she had seen him shoot the assailant point-blank in the head.

Minutes later, he made a joke about some armchair.

"I don't understand how you could go from killing a man to commenting about an armchair." Sienna turned away to look outside the window.

Interstate 75 was jam packed with rush hour traffic going north, but they were spared from the congestion since their van was going south toward the airport.

Sienna glanced at the driver. Other than the lawsuit remark, he hadn't said any other word to either one of them.

"Does he know where to take us?" Sienna asked.

Earl nodded. "We'll stay overnight at a safe house until the FBI debriefs us, and then we'll fly to the conference in Savannah."

Sienna closed her eyes. "Maybe I don't want to go. I don't need to do this anymore. I was told I could go straight into WITSEC even without this last task."

"That's why I'm here," Earl said softly. "I'll make sure you're okay."

"No." Sienna glared at him. "You cannot guarantee my safety. I should never have called Helen Hu."

Then again, she had no one else to turn to. She had known Helen since they were kids. Helen Hu's mother and Sienna's mother had done some business together. When Sienna found out that Helen was now world famous for her private investigator successes, she'd called, hoping to only get a piece of advice on how to proceed.

Instead, Helen had immediately sent this dude Sienna had never met before—all the way from Savannah, the hometown she hadn't visited in years. Next thing she knew, the FBI found out she had called Helen Hu. And lo and behold, they agreed to let Earl be a part of the ruse.

Because of his special skills, they said. Whatever they were.

Two disposable civilians.

Sienna closed her eyes. "I should have stayed with Dana. I'm a familiar face."

"I don't think the paramedics would let you get close if they're busy working on her," Earl said.

"Am I next?" Sienna asked.

Earl was silent.

"Am I?" Sienna asked again.

"I don't want to scare you. The truth is, I don't know."

"Then I'll tell you, Earl. If we don't take down GOOP, I'll be dead."

CHAPTER THREE

"That bad, huh?" Helen Hu was sipping coffee in her office in Athens, Greece, as she listened to Earl talk about his afternoon gone awry.

Earl had gotten out of the shower and changed into a T-shirt and track pants, making himself at home in the safe house. After he talked to Helen, he would go downstairs to see if the debriefing was over. Somewhere at the back of his mind, he wondered if it had been wise to leave Sienna with FBI Special Agent Perez downstairs, but he was sure Sienna was in good hands.

While he had been in the shower, Agent Kimball had texted him to let him know that his SUV had been delivered to the safe house and was in the garage two floors down. He texted back to say he appreciated being a part of the project.

Kimball didn't reply.

On the laptop screen in front of him on a small desk in his assigned bedroom, Earl could see pretty much the entire wall behind the table where Helen was sitting, including a giant clock. It was past three o'clock in the morning over there. He regretted calling her so late in the night, but then she was still wide awake.

To Earl, it made no sense for Helen to handle things stateside, to cover for him while he was away on an undercover mission. Thing was, neither of them could trust any of the other Hu Knows, Inc., employees to take charge of the Savannah headquarters while he was out here in Atlanta, keeping Sienna safe from unknown enemies. However, with Hugo in Brussels and Helen in Athens, there was no one else in charge of their Savannah office except Earl.

Helen liked to run her offices lean and mean. In other words, shorthanded.

"As soon as we find out who would kill to prevent her from whistleblowing, the sooner this will be over," Earl said. "And then I'll be back in Savannah and you can go back to your normal sleep pattern."

Helen Hu nodded. "I put you in this situation."

"She's... It's like..." Earl couldn't put his thoughts together.

"I'm sorry. I thought you could handle her better than Cade can."

Cade Summer. A new hire at Hu Knows, Inc., he strutted around like he knew beans about beans the moment he earned his PI license.

"I didn't send him to Atlanta. He's single and looking for a date. Sienna might be uncomfortable," Helen said.

Earl wasn't sure what to make of it. He was single too. What was Helen saying? "Strangely enough, I think we're a good fit—her friend thought we were actually dating before we even said anything."

"Go on."

"What?"

"You sound like you wanted to say something else."

"Like what?"

"I don't know. She's a very sweet lady or something?"

"She's slightly paranoid and uh..."

"When was the last time you were tongue-tied?" Helen chuckled. "Were you going to say that she's distracted?"

Earl shrugged. "She doesn't sit still and she doesn't trust the FBI—and possibly me."

"You have until next weekend." Helen smiled. "One week at an oceanfront resort in the Bahamas, all expenses paid. And another week off after that on Tybee Island."

The second week off had sweetened the deal for Earl. Maybe. Then again, it would be a staycation. "A resort twenty minutes away from my own house. Woo hoo."

"Free is free."

"That's what I keep telling myself." Earl prayed he wouldn't regret taking up the assignment. How hard could it be? His Special Ops training from long ago and the many years of PI work since then had prepared him for this. Besides, staying at a five-star hotel and eating for free were too appealing to pass up.

He had even packed two pairs of swimming trunks to alternate so that one could dry while he swam in the other. He should have brought two pairs of flip-flops and packed more sunblock lotion, but whatever.

"By the way, when you get there, if you see Donovan Moss, you might want to say hello. Keep us on his mind," Helen said. "He has connections worldwide. We could always use new clients who can pay."

It was typical of Helen to remind him that it was a business trip, not quite a vacation. The last time he had an all-expenses paid vacation was when he was shot up badly while on assignment in California. He missed the rest of the adventure that his friend, FBI Special Agent Jake Kessler, was on, but Earl did get a month off, lazing on the beach on Tybee Island while recuperating from his wounds.

Earl remembered Donovan, the brother of Byron Moss, one of the pastors at Midtown Chapel in Atlanta that Earl attended whenever he was in town. Midtown Chapel was a sister church to Riverside Chapel in Savannah, Earl's home church. And Byron had married one of the former members of Riverside.

"Does he know what is going on next week?" Earl asked.

"I'm sure the FBI has briefed him on it," Helen said. "Has Cora said anything to you?"

"No." Earl wouldn't have missed her call.

Corazon Garcia-Moss used to moonlight for Hu Knows until she met and married Donovan. She moved to Nassau to become his chief of security at all the Moss hotels worldwide, including their newest acquisition, an oceanfront resort on Tybee Island which they had named Moss Tybee.

"You might want to check in with her once you land at Freeport," Helen suggested.

Earl nodded. "And I'll stay close to Sienna."

"Don't worry. It's just for one week."

"That's what I've been telling myself. It'll all be over in a week—if Sienna doesn't get herself killed." Earl expelled a breath. "She came within seconds of death this afternoon."

"Yeah, you told me. I wish she were more forthcoming about where she's going or what she's doing instead of winging it."

"Does she wing things a lot?" Earl asked.

"You tell me. She seems to plan things on the fly. That's how I see it." Helen tried to pour more coffee out of a carafe but it was empty. She shrugged. "Speaking of flying, when do you fly out?"

"Eight, but we have to be at the airport by six for security. We change planes in Fort Lauderdale before heading out to Freeport," Earl said. "I wish we could put her on a private jet, but that would surely arouse suspicions."

"Right. You don't want her boss to think something fishy is going on." Helen yawned. "Keep me posted, and keep tabs on your expenses."

Earl nodded. "I don't know why you're doing her this favor, Helen. It's very expensive. I mean, sure, you knew each other from way back when."

"It's not a favor. Her uncle, Tabbebo Jennings, is footing the bill."

"Oh." That, Earl didn't know. He leaned back.

"He doesn't want his favorite niece killed."

"It would cost him a fortune to keep her alive."

"Yeah. The Sienna I knew all my life is super independent, so when she asked for help, it meant she was either way in over her head or second-guessing herself."

"Or both." Earl sighed. "I wish she would talk to me, tell me what she's going to do *before* she does it."

"Obviously something is very wrong at GOOP," Helen said. "When her boyfriend was shot in the back and killed in the parking lot, but his wallet and laptop were not stolen, that raised a red flag—especially when the local police ruled it as a robbery homicide before the investigation was complete."

There were multiple red flags. When Earl took up the assignment, FBI Special Agent Mariana Kimball told him that the deceased had once been an FBI informant. They went after his girlfriend. Sienna knew some things, but not enough hard evidence against her CEO. So they made a deal with her. If she could be their eyes and ears at GOOP, then her boyfriend's death would not have been in vain.

Considering how little Sienna revealed about what she knew, Earl suspected that she knew more than she let on. Either that, or she really had no idea.

"The fact that her boyfriend was murdered scared her," Helen said. "Sienna believes she was getting careless and that someone was going after her. That's the real reason she called."

"After this afternoon, I might agree with her." Earl laughed.

Helen pointed a finger at the camera. "That was your fault. You should never have left her side."

Like right now.

"Her friend wouldn't talk," Earl defended himself. "I agreed to wait outside for five minutes—though it went longer. When I saw the active shooter, he had killed the FBI agent waiting in his vehicle, and was heading toward the kitchen window."

"You told me you were hiding in the bushes. No need to rehash it all."

"I barely made it inside the house. One more

second, and you'd be attending your friend's funeral."

Helen nodded. "What did Agent Kimball say?"

"She doesn't like Sienna, doesn't trust her, doesn't want to have anything to do with her."

"Funny she'd tell you that."

"I read between the lines."

"I sent you to Atlanta because you've worked with the FBI field office there."

"I get around."

"I bet. Your Rolodex runneth over."

Earl shrugged. "Might never know when I need a favor."

"Do you trust Kimball?" Helen asked.

"Yeah, I trust her."

"Friends?"

"Acquaintances."

"You tried to ask her out."

"She turned me down every time."

"I need someone professional, and I know I can count on you not to fall in love with Agent Kimball... or Sienna, for that matter."

"What are you talking about?" Earl sat up straight.

"I'm just warning you. God is watching."

"You're going spiritual on me, Helen."

"The God factor makes all the difference in the

world," Helen said. "Speaking of Whom, please pray for Sienna. She's in a dark place right now. How's her colleague Dana doing?"

"I'll check after we're done here." Earl wondered too.

"When do you get your debriefing?"

"Done," Earl said. "Perez talked to me while Sienna was in the shower."

"You locked her in?" Helen laughed.

"You know I can't. She's not a caged animal."

"Of course not, but you might want to check sooner than later."

"You know something I don't?" Earl was going to get out of his chair this instant.

"You know my mom."

Earl nodded. "With all due respect, Mama Hu is a very colorful character."

"With a criminal past—for which she is serving time. How do you think my mom knows Sienna's mom?"

"Never crossed my mind."

"Sienna's mother is a master thief and escape artist."

"No." Earl reached for his phone in a corner, where it was being charged up. He logged in and checked his app. The GPS tracker said that Sienna's purse was still in her room.

That might not be good enough.

"I need to run, Helen." Earl was on his feet, looking for his flip-flops. "I better go check on Sienna."

"Take care and have fun at the conference."

"Yeah, sure." Earl logged out of his laptop. Debated whether to pack up now.

Yes, I better.

But first, he had to see if the interview was over. He padded downstairs.

All was quiet.

He peeked into the home office. No one there. The interview must have been over, unless Perez took Sienna to another part of the house.

He checked the living room. No one was there.

The kitchen was empty. All the lights were on.

He heard a groan that seemed to come from the other side of the counter. He rushed around the peninsula, and there on the floor was Agent Perez, holding her head—right next to a frying pan.

"What the..." Earl was on his knees. "Perez, are you hurt?"

"Is that a stupid question?" She groaned. Touched the back of her head again. "Man, she gave me a goose egg."

"She? Sienna? How did you know it was her?"

"Either it was her or you. Do you see anyone else here?"

"I was in my room, talking to my boss." Earl helped her up.

She wobbled on her feet. "She was going upstairs, so she asked for your SUV key to give to you on her way to her bedroom."

"How nice of her."

Perez moaned. "I turned away for a second—and bam!"

Earl rushed to the kitchen door leading to the garage. He suspected what he would find when he opened that door. Sure enough, one spot was empty in the two-car garage.

He had one more tracker. He swiped his phone. Sure enough, his SUV was at least five miles away.

He turned around. "May I borrow your vehicle?"

"No. I'm coming with you." Perez staggered.

"You might not be in a condition to drive."

Perez threw the SUV key to Earl. "Who says I'm driving?"

"All right. I'll drive and you call Kim." Realizing he was wearing flip-flops on his feet, he cringed. "Gimme a minute to change my shoes."

The agent barely nodded, and then collapsed

on the floor. Uh-oh. Earl checked her pulse. Still alive. She might have a concussion, but he wasn't a doctor, so it was a wild guess.

Earl called 911, and gave the location of the safe house. He called Agent Kimball to send someone over there as he ran upstairs two steps at a time.

On the way to his bedroom, he knocked on Sienna's bedroom door. "Sienna?"

No answer.

He had guessed that she wouldn't be there, but he had to check. He turned the knob. It was unlocked. "Sienna?"

There, on the bed, was her dirty purse. It was empty except for the tracking device he had put in the zipped side pocket. Sienna had taken her phone with her.

He checked his own phone. If Sienna was driving his SUV...

There on his tracking app, a moving red dot told Earl that Sienna was driving toward Conyers, which was about thirty minutes from the safe house —if there was no road construction or evening traffic. He had to hurry.

After he pulled on his socks and boots, he grabbed his loaded Glock and ran downstairs. He could hear sirens in the distance. Paramedics were on their way.

He ran past Perez, still on the floor. He opened the garage door and climbed into the unmarked SUV. As he tapped his phone to turn on the navigation app for his tracker, he prayed that Sienna wouldn't do what he wouldn't.

He placed his phone vertically in a cupholder, and backed the SUV out of the garage. He couldn't see any paramedics or fire truck anywhere.

"What are you up to, Sienna?" Earl asked aloud as he drove the vehicle down the road to a nearby intersection.

Just then, a fire truck turned into the road he was leaving.

"Lord, please let Perez be okay." In his rearview mirror, he saw the fire truck stop at the safe house.

CHAPTER FOUR

"Leave me out of this." Sienna's colleague and computer expert handed the whistle back to her. "I shouldn't have let you in. Please leave now."

"Arun, please." Sienna clasped the whistle in her hands. She stood her ground in the foyer of Arun Dhillon's house. She hadn't driven here in a stolen vehicle for nothing.

"It's enough for me to show you that the whistle is a USB drive," Arun said. "Why did Dana give it to you?"

"I don't know. Help me."

Upstairs, a baby cried.

Arun tensed up. "I can't. I have a family now."

"Rocco and I will never have a family together.

In his memory, please help me." Even though Sienna had dated Rocco for only a couple of months before he died, she felt that they had something special. Now they would never know.

Upstairs, the baby's cry grew louder.

"Do you need to check on her?" Sienna asked.

"My wife is, I'm sure. You need to leave now. Go." Arun didn't touch her but he motioned her toward the door.

"Please help me," Sienna pleaded. "I know you can read this USB—"

"No. I don't want the FBI at my door."

"Please."

"If you don't leave, I'll call 911."

Sienna stepped back. "You told me you were going to help."

"Before I found out you talked to the FBI."

"No..." Sienna wondered how to lie without lying. She couldn't do it. Yes, she had talked to the FBI. Yes, she had gone from a whistleblower to an informant.

"If you see Dana, tell her I say hello, okay?" Arun's eyes had that faraway look, as if to say that if things had been different...

"Dana has been shot and she's at the hospital." Sienna put the necklace back around her neck.

"Wh-what did you say?"

"Hours ago. They came for her. They're coming for me... and you too."

Arun's face turned angry. "You're leading them to my house, my family!"

He shoved Sienna out of the front door.

Right into someone's warm torso.

Sienna started to scream, but a large hand cupped over her mouth.

"Shhh. It's me, your knight." He almost chuckled. "Earl. Knight. Get it?"

Sienna sighed. She pushed Earl's hand away. "What are you doing here?"

Before Earl could answer, Arun stepped outside and closed his front door. "Who are you?"

Sienna mumbled something that sounded like *boyfriend*. She still could not wrap her head around the idea of a fake boyfriend. However, her life depended on it—and yet she had run away from him.

The whistle USB must contain important information. It had to. Why else would Dana give it to her? However, Sienna's desire to know what was in there had caused her to make haphazard decisions on the fly that would have been out of character for her at work.

Truth be told, she had never been this disorganized in her life. In the past—before Rocco was gunned down—she had been meticulous about her schedule. Nothing was done unless it was on her calendar of events. Lunch was an event. Snack was an event. Calling her dentist to make an appointment was an event. Drinking water all day long was an event.

After she buried Rocco, Sienna's life had fallen apart. She lost sleep, misplaced things, forgot appointments. Her boss had been forgiving of her. It helped that Mr. Ford had been out of town a lot, giving her an excuse and room to fix her mistakes and cover up her incompetence.

"Boyfriend?" Arun shook his head. "It's not even six months since Rocco died. Whassup, woman?"

"He's dead, I'm alive," Earl explained. "You can't date a dead dude. Now, if you don't want to be dead, you need to help us."

Sienna glanced at Earl. Did he have any idea what she was trying to ask Arun to do for her?

"I'm not doing anything for this woman." Arun stepped inside his house. "I'm going to pack up my family and we're going someplace safe. Don't try to contact us. Please move your vehicle out of my driveway."

He slammed the door in their face.

The porch light went out.

Standing there at the front door in the dark, Sienna wasn't sure what to do.

"Why didn't you wait for me?" Earl asked gently, leading her to his SUV parked in front of the one-car garage, behind Arun's minivan.

"I suppose you want your key back." Sienna reached for her pocket. She could not find the key fob.

Earl dangled it in front of her eyes. "You left it on the driveway outside the driver's side door."

"I did?" Sienna was shocked. The key fob must have fallen out of her hand in her hurry. She remembered being more worried about the whistle.

On the driveway, though?

"Yes, you did," Earl said.

"I'm sorry. I wasn't thinking." Sienna couldn't believe it. "Someone could have driven off with your vehicle."

"Like you did?" Earl opened the passenger side door. "Get in."

"How did you get here?" Sienna asked.

Earl pointed to a dark-colored SUV parked at the curb near the mailbox. It looked like the other vehicle in the safe house garage.

"How did you find me?" Sienna asked.

Earl didn't answer. He went around his SUV and got in, then started the engine. He backed out of the short driveway. As Earl reversed the vehicle onto the dark road, Sienna heard the garage door open.

Arun ran out, carrying a diaper bag and rolling a suitcase. He unlocked his minivan and put the suitcase in the back.

"How did he pack so quickly?" Earl asked.

"Maybe he has already packed."

Earl nodded. "That means he knows something's going on at GOOP."

"Should I try to talk to him again?" Sienna asked.

"No." Earl put his SUV in gear.

Sienna watched her colleague close the back door of the van, go to the driver's seat, climb in, and—

The explosion was deafening. The van lifted in the air, and slammed down on the concrete driveway again. Sienna screamed as she watched flames engulf the charred van.

Earl hit the gas pedal.

"Stop!" Sienna slapped the dashboard. "We have to help him!"

"I don't think we can help him." Earl tossed her his phone. "Call 911. They can get help here. Whoever tried to kill him might also be after you."

"He can't be dead."

"He was inside a vehicle that exploded. Trust me, he's dead." Earl floored the gas pedal out of the subdivision.

Sienna's hand shook so much she could not hold the phone.

"Calm down and call 911. I can't because Georgia Law says I can't drive and talk on the phone."

"Where's your hands-free dock?" Sienna asked.

"It's broken. I meant to get it fixed but here we are."

Sienna drew a deep breath. She tapped the emergency button on Earl's phone and talked to the dispatcher. After she gave the address, she hung up.

"You know they're going to track down your phone," Sienna said.

"Are they?" Earl merged into traffic. "Why did you leave the safe house?"

"I had no choice."

"You assaulted a federal agent," Earl said as they went down the road.

"Is she okay?"

"She was passed out when I left her. I had to call 911."

Sienna blinked. She didn't recall hitting Agent Perez that hard. "I'm sorry. Will I be arrested?"

"Probably, but right now we need to keep you alive. What spooked you?"

"She asked me strange questions that have nothing to do with Mr. Ford."

"Like what?"

Sienna didn't want to tell him. Maybe later. "Suffice to say that I didn't have a good feeling about Agent Perez."

"So you left."

"They dropped off your SUV key. It was right there on the counter."

"Then you bashed her on the head with a frying pan and took off to see your colleague. What for?" Earl asked. "Tell me the truth."

Sienna drew a deep breath, closed her eyes, and counted to ten. Then twenty. Thirty.

"Tell me the truth and I can help you," Earl said.

Sienna opened her eyes. "Would you?"

"That's what you hired me to do."

"Technically, my uncle paid for your services. If it were up to me, I wouldn't have."

"You called Helen," Earl reminded her.

"Yes, I did, but I couldn't afford her and she doesn't do pro bono work." Sienna looked away. Outside, shops and gas stations came and went as

Earl headed back to the highway in the opposite direction she had come from.

"Neither does she give discounts. So who called your uncle?" Earl drove the vehicle onto the Interstate 20 ramp.

"Helen didn't say. My guess is that she called my uncle, who is my mom's full-time caregiver. He's retired and lives on social security. I don't know where he got the money to pay Helen."

"Where do they live?"

"Chattanooga."

"Do you get to see them often?"

Sienna shook her head. "I try to go up there every other month to see Mom, but in the last several months, I've stayed away. I need this problem solved, Earl. Do you understand? Then I can go back to my normal life."

"Then tell me the truth, Sienna."

"Where are you taking me?" Interstate 20 could keep going all the way through Atlanta, and then western Georgia to Alabama.

"I'm going to get on 285, and drive round and round until you tell me what's going on," Earl said. "Otherwise I cannot help you."

Before Sienna could put her thoughts into words, Earl's phone buzzed.

"Agent Kimball." He tapped his phone to call her back. Audio only. "Yes, ma'am?"

"I heard," Kimball said over the speakerphone.

"Any word?" Earl asked.

"A dead man in the driver's seat."

Sienna gasped. "His wife and child?"

"They were safe inside the house. I'm on my way to interview them," Kimball said. "I need you to get Sienna to the new safe house pronto."

"What happened to the old safe house?"

"Perez is dead," Kimball said over the speakerphone. "It's a crime scene now."

In the passenger seat, Sienna was beside herself. "Oh no. I'm sorry. I didn't hit her that hard. The pan was aluminum, not even steel."

"The real Perez has been dead before you two arrived at the safe house," Kimball said. "The woman whose head you bashed disappeared before the ambulance arrived."

"She passed out on the floor when I left," Earl said.

"She must've been pretending." Kimball drew a deep breath.

"What's her name?" Earl asked.

"Joy Burditt. Goes by Killjoy," Kimball said.

"And you figured it out this quickly. How?"

"Fingerprints everywhere. She's in the NCIC.

Wanted in five states for murder. Multiple outstanding federal warrants."

Earl whistled. "How did she find the safe house?"

"Someone let her in while we were extracting you from Dana's house," Kimball said.

"What is NCIC?" Sienna asked.

"The National Crime Information Center database," Earl replied.

Kimball moved on. "Go to Sandy Springs. When you get there, call me. I'll tell you where the safe house is. I need you two to go straight there. I think Killjoy is out looking for you."

"Yes. Ma'am."

Sienna prayed quickly for the right words to say. "Which hospital did they take Dana to?"

No one answered.

"You heard the lady," Earl said.

"She's at Grady," Kimball finally replied.

"How's her baby?" Sienna asked.

"Baby?"

"Yes, ma'am. Back at the house, she told me she was pregnant."

"Whose baby?" Kimball asked.

"I don't know for sure, but she gave me the impression it was Mr. Ford's." That was all Sienna knew. She prayed for Dana that she and the baby would be well.

"Good to know," Kimball replied. "Now put on your seat belt. I don't want you going through the windshield in a wreck."

Sienna's jaw dropped. She pulled her safety belt over her shoulder. "How did you know I wasn't..."

Earl didn't say a word. He simply shook his head. "Hey, Agent Kimball."

"Yes, Earl?"

"Neither Sienna and I have eaten. We're going to grab a bite on the way."

"Get takeout." Kimball's voice was harsh.

"I know a safe place near the Galleria." Earl glanced at Sienna. "We'll do a little detour to Sandy Springs."

"All right," Kimball said. "I know I'm going to regret this already."

"You know where we are," Earl said.

"Yes, we do."

"Then you can keep us safe, right?" Earl laughed.

Kimball laughed with him and hung up.

CHAPTER FIVE

"Something is not right," Sienna said.

Earl didn't answer. He reached over to hold Sienna's hand. "Don't worry. I'm on your side."

Just before Highway 20 intersected with Interstate 285, Earl pulled over into a gas station. "That's a good price for gas. I'll fill up the tank."

Sienna looked up at the sign. That was not a good price at all. In fact, it was two cents more than some other gas stations. Not only that, there was still half a tank of gas left in the SUV.

She wasn't sure what Earl was up to. She waited as Earl filled the gas tank while he stood outside the vehicle, tapping away at his phone. He had a worried look on his face. Then he started moving his phone back and forth across the doors of the SUV.

What on earth was he doing?

Sienna prayed that God would keep them safe. She leaned against the headrest and closed her eyes. The day had been overwhelming, to say the least.

To begin with, she'd hardly had any sleep the night before. By three in the morning, she had packed her suitcase for the conference on Grand Bahama Island in the Bahamas. She mostly filled it with summer clothes, shoes, and sunblock. Then she tried to go back to sleep, but the recurring flashbacks of how Rocco had died filled her with fear and anxiety.

She had gone to work immediately in her home office, even as her first pot of coffee of the day was brewing in her kitchen. By the time Earl knocked on her front door with takeout Chinese food, it was noon, and she couldn't remember all that she had gotten done and hadn't gotten done.

She heard the vehicle door shut, and Sienna opened her eyes. She turned her head toward the driver's side as Earl started the SUV.

"Do you remember when we first met?" Earl asked.

"How can you make small talk like that?" Sienna asked. "Arun's dead."

"Sometimes it's good to talk about something else. Humor me."

Sienna closed her eyes. A tear trickled. So much going on. It was confusing.

"Wasn't it last week?" Earl asked.

Sienna nodded.

"We hit it off right away. You weren't afraid of me."

"Should I be?" Sienna asked.

"I don't know. Sometimes people say I'm intimidating." Earl pulled out of the gas station.

"Is it because of your height?"

"You're pretty tall yourself. In fact, you're one of the tallest ladies I've dated...uh..."

"Look at you, playing the boyfriend role already. Mr. Ford would totally believe that we're in a relationship with each other."

Earl chuckled. "I'm good at playing the part."

"If circumstances were different..."

"Go on."

Sienna shook her head. "I'm tired and not thinking straight."

"Really? Or were you trying to ask me if we could be friends outside of this trouble bubble?"

Sienna had to think about his question. "I don't know."

Southbound Interstate 285 was filled with brake lights.

"It's almost ten. I'm surprised we still have traffic," Earl said.

"At least we have a full tank of gas."

"For sure."

Sienna looked outside the window. "You know, I can't remember how many times I've pleaded to God for help in the last six months."

"God sent help, didn't He?" Earl eased into traffic on the southbound Interstate 285.

"You mean you?"

"I could very well be a part of your support team. Helen, your uncle, me. And your praying friends at your church at Lakeside."

"So you know where I go to church in metro Atlanta." Sienna figured he had probably read up about her. "What else do you know about me?"

"That you're in big trouble, but you're too proud to receive help."

"Am I proud?" Sienna hadn't been able to do any self-evaluation. The many sleepless nights had affected her ability to think straight. "I need answers."

"And Arun Dhillon had the answers?" Earl

changed lanes. It turned out that one lane was blocked due to a fender bender. Police cars and two fire trucks were at the scene, as was a tow truck.

"I didn't tell you his name."

"Agent Kimball and I looked up his address."

"How did you follow me...oh... You have a tracker in your SUV."

"This is a company vehicle. Never know when someone might just drive off in it."

"You don't trust me," Sienna said, stating the obvious. After all, she had taken his vehicle without permission.

"Do you trust me?" Earl asked.

Sienna was silent. She wasn't sure. "Helen wants me to trust you."

"Then trust me." Earl reached out for Sienna's hand.

She let him hold it. His hand was warm.

"If you don't trust me—yet—then how about trusting God for me?" Earl asked.

"Good idea. To tell you the truth, I'm afraid of what might happen to me, to my family."

"All the more reason to trust God," Earl said softly. "Pray Psalm 56:3 back to Him. 'Whenever I am afraid, I will trust in You.' Okay?"

Sienna nodded. "Do you usually hold the hand of your clients?"

"Not unless we're pretending to be in a relationship. We might as well practice."

"We're in a vehicle by ourselves. No one else is here." Sienna waved her other hand in the air.

"At this time tomorrow night, we'll need to convince your boss that we are together, or this whole thing will blow up and I can't help you anymore."

"I feel like we're getting somewhere, but if GOOP blows up..." Sienna couldn't finish her sentence.

"Good administrative assistants are sought after."

Sienna shook her head. "A whistleblower cannot be trusted. I'd be earning peanuts—no offense to peanut growers."

"You could change your career. Or get retraining. Money is not everything."

"My mother has dementia and is living with her widowed brother. But you knew that."

Earl nodded.

"As an administrative assistant, I have to work extra to earn enough to pay for her daily care. I don't have enough left over to pay Helen. I had to sell my house, buy a smaller car, emptied out all my savings just to keep Mom alive."

"I'm sorry."

"Nothing to do with you." Sienna shifted in her passenger seat. "I work a lot of overtime. Sometimes Mr. Ford works late, and I'm there until he's done. I hear things, I see things. Too much."

"Do y'all call him Mr. Ford all the time?" Earl asked.

"He's only ten years older than I am, but it's a safety wall between us, you know?" Sienna smiled. "He hated me calling him Mr. Ford. He said it makes him feel twenty years older than I am. Dana called him Finnegan, even at work."

Earl put his blinker on and changed lanes. Sienna could not believe they were heading on Interstate 75 North already.

"For two years, I ignored whatever was happening," Sienna continued. "Then I met Teo. He was charming and sweet—a perfect gentleman. For a whole year, he worked at GOOP. During that time, he dumped me and cozied up to Dana."

"I'm sorry."

"Teo and I were not a good fit. He was better off with Dana." Sienna sniffled. "She's my friend, but she can be stubborn. They talked about kids and she wanted five and he wanted three. She quit smoking on account of him."

"Until one day..."

"Will you let me tell the story?" Sienna

snapped. "Yes, then one day he was fired. We found out that he had been taking photographs of documents which would be sent over to GOOP's competitors. After that, Dana and I became close, like sisters. She paid for lunch at work every day so I could be an attentive listener to her problems—lamentations, I call them. Truth be told, I would have listened anyway even if I took care of my own lunch."

"I feel sorry for her already."

"Pretty soon, Arun joined us and we became friends. Turned out, he'd been interested in Dana too—why isn't anyone interested in me?—and she was getting lonely. He suggested she spend more time in the gym—with him, you see."

Earl nodded.

"She was at the company gym one day and ran into Mr. Ford, who had just had a fight with his wife of many years. He had gone to the gym to blow off steam, and there was Dana in the rooftop pool outside the gym. They were the only people in the pool that evening. And so it began."

"How long did Dana and Mr. Ford have their affair?" Earl asked.

"Until Mr. Ford's wife found out. Then she filed for divorce. They didn't have a prenup. She walked away with nineteen billion dollars."

Earl whistled. "That must've caused a financial chain reaction for Mr. Ford."

"Not anymore. He slept with one of the GOOP partners, and persuaded her to sell her shares to him. Now he owns fifty-five percent of the company."

"Did that make the other partners mad?"

"It made Sandrina Owens mad because Mr. Ford dumped her afterwards. She took him to court, but the sale was legit. She moved out of state after that," Sienna said. "They kept Owens in the company name."

"What about the other partners?" Earl asked.

"Mr. Ford's half brother, Zachary Gavard, is the 'G' in the company name. He owns twenty-five percent of GOOP. 'Furious' can't even begin to describe him." Sienna recalled the day Gavard stormed into Mr. Ford's office and broke a glass wall. "He's got anger management problems."

Earl turned on his blinker to merge into traffic going north on Interstate 85. Someone honked at him.

"Eyes on the road, Mr. Young," Sienna ordered.

"Yes, dear. So between Ford and Gavard, they own eighty percent of GOOP. Who owns the remaining twenty percent?"

"Ten percent belongs to Mr. Gavard's wife, Celestia, née Oppenheimer."

"Ah, the other 'O' in the name."

"Another ten percent is distributed among other investors—who are going to be at the private conference next week at Moss Grand Bahama."

"Tell me this," Earl said. "Who runs the company if something happens to Mr. Ford?"

"Mr. Gavard and Celestia."

"If something happens to Mr. Gavard?"

"Celestia would own ninety percent of the whole shebang," Sienna said.

Earl whistled. "What does Celestia do?"

"I don't know, to be honest. All I know is that she does show up at the quarterly company meetings, and she knows many of GOOP's investors."

"Back to Arun..." Earl said.

Siena burst into tears. "Sorry."

"Don't be." Earl pointed to the glove compartment. "There's some paper napkins in there."

Sienna nodded. After she blew her nose with the paper napkins from Krispy Kreme, she tried to answer Earl's question. "What did you want to know about Arun?"

"When Arun lost Dana to Mr. Ford, what did he do?"

"Disappointed, Arun married someone else and

they now have a child. Then Dana broke up with Mr. Ford, but it was too late. Arun told me privately that he could not have gone back to a woman who would sleep with someone else's husband. Of course, I could never tell Dana what he said."

"Interesting," Earl said quietly, but Sienna heard him.

"What?"

"That people confided in you. You must listen well."

Sienna felt uneasy hearing Earl's comment, like she had spoken too much. Then she remembered how Agent Kimball had seen her not wearing a seat belt. There must be a camera in front of her, but she could not see it.

She wondered if she should say something to Earl. He seemed nonchalant about it. He had asked her to trust him. It was too late for her to back out now.

She decided that this wasn't the time to tell Earl about the whistle USB drive. Instead, she prayed to God for wisdom and timing.

She needed both more than ever.

CHAPTER SIX

Yeah, something wasn't right.

Earl felt it in his gut, but he could not explain it to himself, let alone to anyone else asking. All he knew was that gnawing feeling that something was wrong, and that the FBI might have been infiltrated, with an assassin in the safe house.

He recalled an event a few years back, when he had helped FBI Special Agent Jake Kessler catch a terrorist. Their enemy had consistently caught up with them no matter where they went. At the end of the day, it turned out that the FBI had a mole working for the terrorist organization.

Had the mole been excised?

As soon as he had a moment, Earl would text

Jake to find out. Not right now, not when he was driving.

He glanced over at the passenger seat to find Sienna crying softly. He had no more tissues to hand to her. She had used up his entire stash of Krispy Kreme paper napkins. He prayed silently for the poor woman.

They were twenty minutes out to the Chinese restaurant. He expected Deshon Kernaghan to drop off the vehicle and his burner phone any minute now, and then return to housesit for Sienna. The Marine Corps reservist moonlighted for Hu Knows, Inc., on occasion when the need arose.

This time, Earl wished he hadn't come to Atlanta alone. However, Helen Hu operated a lean-and-mean headquarters in Savannah, having branched out to new offices in Europe. Helen had hinted that she was closing their branch in Brussels —meaning that Hugo would be moving to the Athens office or moved home to Savannah.

As much as he liked Hugo, Earl did not think the Savannah office could handle two bosses. Ironically, at this moment, Earl could use all the help he could get from Hugo, his old friend and colleague.

Cade Sumter was too new and his ego was too big for Earl to partner with. Cade had to work alone—or go through a fiery furnace a few times—to learn to play well with others in the PI firm. Yet Helen refused to fire him.

Between Cade and Deshon, Earl would take Deshon any day. However, Deshon did not want to leave the police force and work full time for Helen Hu. They had met, and Deshon refused to give any opinion of Helen. He neither liked nor disliked her.

That meant Deshon didn't like Helen enough to want to work for her.

And so here was Earl, working alone.

Interstate 75 going north was still filled with vehicles, although the traffic wasn't at a standstill.

Sienna was still awake, but she didn't say a word. Maybe she knew she shouldn't.

As clear as day, Agent Kimball had planted a hidden camera inside his SUV. Earl didn't like that because Kimball hadn't asked for his permission to do so.

Then again, there was nothing to hide, was there? Earl had called Kimball to tell her where Arun's house was in Conyers—so that she could pick up the FBI vehicle parked outside Arun's house.

Earl took the exit for Cobb Galleria, then made another turn down a surface road toward the Chinese restaurant, where he expected Deshon to not only leave him a vehicle, but a takeout for two inside the vehicle.

It seemed presumptuous of him to know what Sienna wanted, but while he had been waiting for the gas tank to fill up back at the station, Earl had ordered what Sienna ordered the week before. Bits of information like that which Helen had provided for him came from expensive sources. Data would explain why Hu Knows was too costly for the average Joe to hire.

Earl wondered how Sienna's uncle would be able to foot the bill if he was on fixed income. At seventy-nine years old, Tabbebo Jennings had seen plenty of life behind him. Perhaps he had dipped into his savings to pay the required deposit for Helen to send someone to Atlanta to protect his niece.

What of the balance?

Well, what was the price of a human life?

By the time they reached Chop de Chop, Sienna had dozed off. Earl eased his SUV past valet parking to the side of the restaurant building. As if on cue, a man in a baseball cap and face mask waved to him from the parking lot.

Deshon.

He walked away from Earl and a small car flashed its headlights once.

Earl drove away from the small vehicle and parked at the edge of the parking lot, right behind a tow truck. Deshon was nearby somewhere.

Earl called her name to wake her up. He gently touched her arm.

Sienna stirred. She looked exhausted.

"Let's go," Earl said quietly to Sienna. "Dinnertime."

Sienna nodded, reaching for her phone that apparently had slipped from her hands and onto the floorboard while she had been sleeping.

Earl reached over the center panel and took the phone from her. He placed it gently back on the floorboard.

"What are you doing?" Sienna asked.

Earl wasn't sure how to explain it. He needed a distraction, in case Agent Kimball was still watching them from the cameras she had installed on the dashboard, which he hoped couldn't see the floorboard. Deshon would take care of their phones in a minute.

His fingers gently caressed Sienna's jawline.

She closed her eyes.

However, Earl did not kiss her.

Sienna opened her eyes. "You wanted to."

Earl sighed. "Yes."

"Why didn't you?"

"Because... Uh..."

"Take two." She closed her eyes again.

Startled at a side of Sienna that wasn't in the dossier that Helen had put together, Earl froze for a second before reaching for her face again. He kissed her on her cheek and then whispered in her ear, "Leave the phone."

Earl reached between the seats and grabbed his messenger bag with his laptop inside. He was glad he had remembered to bring the bag with him when he left the safe house near the airport, and had put it into his SUV at Arun's house when he found that Sienna had left his vehicle unlocked.

Sienna exited the vehicle without her phone. Earl knew then that she trusted him.

Good. Maybe they would survive this misadventure yet.

"Why are you bringing your bag?" Sienna asked.

"You mean my man purse?"

"Ah. Sorry."

Earl did not nod to Deshon, who also didn't acknowledge him. Earl walked Sienna down the parking lot toward the restaurant before making a sudden turn toward the little car that Deshon had left for him.

Earl leaned toward Sienna's ear. "Do you trust me?"

Sienna nodded.

Earl opened the passenger side door. He pointed to a floppy hat on the seat. "Please put the hat on. And your safety belt."

He went around the car, tossed his messenger bag in the back seat, where he spotted a takeout bag. Then he sat down on the driver's seat. The key was in the ignition. A baseball cap was hanging over the gearshift. He put the cap on, and then his own safety belt.

When he looked over to Sienna, she was grinning. "Got mine on, okay?"

In a compartment between the seats, Earl found a burner phone. He pocketed it.

He started the ignition as he watched Deshon wheel his SUV up the ramp of the tow truck. They couldn't risk leaving the SUV in the parking lot, just in case Agent Kimball sent someone to tail them. Earl had told Deshon to get the SUV out of here, drive off somewhere to disable the trackers and camera, and then tow it to a garage somewhere. Earl would deal with it later.

Right now, there were many unanswered questions.

"Now we can talk." Earl drove the car out of

the Chop de Chop parking lot using a back way, away from the tow truck.

"You don't trust Agent Kimball, do you?" Sienna asked.

"I don't know yet."

"She has a dashcam or secret camera or something in your SUV."

Earl nodded. "She knew you were in Conyers before I got there and told her."

"She didn't come after me, though."

"If she had, would you still have driven to Arun's house?" Earl asked.

"No, probably not. So she's following me around to see where I go and what I do?"

"Like I am?"

"Technically, Agent Kimball could have assigned an undercover FBI agent to be my fake boyfriend."

"Department cutbacks. Not enough human resources," Earl explained.

"Or I'm not high-profile enough?"

"Or maybe I can do things that FBI agents can't do."

"Like what?"

"No red tape for me."

"To skirt the law?"

"Obviously not. Everything we do needs to

hold up in court," Earl said as they stopped at a red light.

"Where are you taking me?" Sienna looked outside.

"You tell me." Earl made his way onto Interstate 285 heading east.

"Why are we getting back on the perimeter?" Sienna asked.

"Tell me why you went to see Arun, and I'll tell you where you'll find the answer you seek."

"The answer I seek?" Sienna chuckled. "Are we on a quest?"

"Arun Dhillon was tech support at GOOP. Is that why you went to see him?"

"Why don't you put two and two together, Mr. Brilliant?" Sienna looked outside.

"If you don't tell me everything, how can I help you?"

"No one can help me."

"God can."

"Except Him. I thought the FBI could help me, but I was almost killed at Dana's house, and they came for me inside the house." Sienna's tone was one of disappointment rather than anger.

"You should have told Agent Kimball yourself."

"You told them anyway, Earl."

"Well, only after you made me sit outside in the

bushes."

Sienna laughed. "I did not tell you to go sit in the bushes. You made the decision yourself."

"Well, I had to be close to the house."

"And you made yourself useful by calling the FBI." Sienna's shoulders sagged. "Thank you, though. I would've died had you not shown up in time."

"God protected us," Earl said. "Now tell me. Did you have something that only Arun could do for you?"

"Like what?"

"You said you trust me." Earl put his blinker on to change lanes as they crossed over the Chattahoochee River. "Prove it."

Sienna drew a deep breath. "Give me a minute."

Earl nodded. They drove on in silence—no music, no radio, just the traffic noises around them —as Earl took them up Highway 400 toward Alpharetta.

He had already guessed that Sienna needed computer help of some sort because she had gone to Arun, the IT guy. Earl could be fifty percent wrong, but he could also be fifty percent right.

Either way, they could stay with Cayson Yang until they figured out their next move. Hopefully the next step would manifest itself before six o'clock in the morning or they'd miss their flight to Savannah. If they missed their flight, they'd have to drive five hours one way.

He prayed that Sienna would open up and be transparent with him. "I'm paid to help you, not anyone else. Let me help."

Sienna didn't respond.

"I'll go first," Earl said. "There were bugs, trackers, cameras, whatnots in my SUV. They were tracking us, wherever we go. From my past experience, I know that sometimes the FBI has moles."

"What?" Sienna sounded surprised.

"Nothing manmade is foolproof, as we know."

"Well, yeah."

"It's not that I don't trust Agent Kimball, but I can't take the risk. Someone had infiltrated the safe house, killed the real Agent Perez."

"Now I don't feel too bad about bashing her head." Sienna paused. "Maybe I do feel bad. She's still a human being."

"I'm sure Agent Kimball would disagree with you."

"Speaking of her, she's going to be mad at us if we don't show up at the new safe house," Sienna suggested.

"If your enemies knew where the first safe

house is, who is to say they don't already know where the next safe house is?"

"Good point."

"I'm going to take you somewhere safe." Earl reached for her hand. She let him hold it.

"What about our flight in the morning?" Sienna asked.

"We'll cross that bridge when we get there."

"Won't Agent Kimball be mad if she finds out that we didn't make it inside the restaurant and we've disappeared all night?"

"It all depends on what you tell me in the next five minutes," Earl said.

He hoped that Sienna would be forthcoming.

"I don't think you can keep the secret much longer," Earl added. "Agent Kimball is probably talking to Arun's wife right now. She might tell her everything she knows if she doesn't want to be handed over to the DHS, get her spouse visa revoked, and sent back to India—her anchor baby notwithstanding."

Sienna straightened up. "How did you know about their visas?"

"There's a reason Hu Knows charges an arm and a leg for its services. Whatever the FBI knows, we will know sooner or later. And remember..."

"You're on my side." Sienna nodded.

CHAPTER SEVEN

S lowly, Sienna pulled out her necklace. She lifted the whistle for Earl to see. He was still driving, so he glanced quickly.

"Dana gave this to me shortly before she was shot," Sienna said.

"Withholding evidence. Your charges are mounting."

"She said it was a gift—belated birthday present."

"Is it?"

"It was odd, but she insisted." Sienna wondered how much to tell him.

"Since you're carrying that around, I gather you did not tell the fake Perez about it at the debriefing," Earl said.

"I couldn't. Isn't that a good thing?"

Earl shook his head. "Amazingly so." Earl shook his head. "Tell me about that whistle."

"This is not a whistle per se," Sienna said. "This is a USB drive. I tried to read it back at the safe house, but it's encrypted. The only person I know in IT is Arun. He was tech support and helped me with my printers and all."

"So you figured a tech guy who knew how to fix printers might be able to read an encrypted USB drive that used to belong to an informant working in a multibillion-dollar company."

"Don't underestimate Arun."

"Don't underestimate your enemies."

"My enemies?" Sienna laughed. "I don't even know who they are or why they're after me."

"Or if they're after you at all."

"Rocco is dead and Dana is in the hospital. The three of us—together with Arun—were lunch buddies," Sienna explained. "Arun used to have a thing for Dana, but her sights were on billionaire Mr. Ford, who took only two years to conquer."

Earl put his blinker on and merged into the light traffic.

Sienna noticed that he was heading east. "Toto, we're not going to Sandy Springs anymore."

"A friend of mine also fixes printers." Earl

chuckled. "He might be able to read your USB drive."

The dashboard clock said it was almost eleven. Time was slow and yet time was fast.

"I hate Friday nights," Sienna blurted.

"Because of what happened tonight?"

"Rocco died on a Friday night too." Sienna's voice cracked. "We had just started dating. Trying to get to know each other. And then it was over."

Earl reached for her hand again.

Sienna could not remember when they had stopped holding hands.

"The sooner we solve this—with God's help— the sooner we'll return to a normal Friday night, okay?" Earl stayed in the right lane.

Sienna nodded.

"What do you usually do on Friday nights?" Earl asked.

Sienna wasn't biting. She did not like personal questions from a stranger. She had no idea how they were going to play their parts at the conference in Savannah, Georgia.

"As for me, I usually go on a date, unless I'm working," Earl answered his own question.

"In which case, you have fake dates."

Earl shrugged. "I'm glad I have a job."

"I won't have one after this."

"I don't mean to..." Earl sighed. "I was trying to make small talk. We have to get to know each other in a matter of hours before the conference."

"Dinner and a movie," Sienna said. "That's what Rocco and I did."

"In a theater?" Earl asked.

"We streamed at home. There's more privacy."

"Your house or your boyfriend's house?"

"Mine, usually. Then we could stay up as late as we wanted, and I didn't have to drive home." Sienna felt awkward speaking of Rocco in the past tense.

"Oh."

"Are you thinking I'm selfish?" Sienna asked.

"I'm thinking you're a Christian woman who has her boyfriend over for an after-dinner movie until late at night."

"I told you we just dated for only a short period."

"Oh sorry. I missed that."

"You're thinking too much." Sienna laughed. "I have a roommate. Her boyfriend came over. He's an associate pastor at my church. Everything is—was—above board."

"That's good."

"Big brother approves?" Sienna asked.

"I'm not your big brother. We're supposed to be an item."

Sienna put her elbow on the armrest of the door. "We're going to get dead."

Earl laughed. "Get dead?"

"Dana. Rocco. Arun. All were going about their normal lives, and then they got into trouble."

"Normal? I think their lives were anything but," Earl said. "Dana pried. Rocco snooped around."

"Like me."

"That's why I'm here." Earl squeezed her hand.

"I wonder how Dana is doing. Do you think she's out of surgery?"

"I'll try to find out for you."

Sienna nodded. "I feel so tired."

"I know. I'm sorry." Earl talked to his phone and ordered it to call someone by the name of Cayson. In seconds, a woman's voice came through.

"Leland?" Earl said. "Where's Cayson?"

"Dead to the world. He passed out tonight. That will happen to anyone who hasn't slept in three days. What's going on?" Leland asked.

"Cayson said I could stop by his office tonight."

"Are you bringing food?"

"We ordered a takeout." Or Deshon ordered for them. "We were going to eat as soon as we get to your office. I ordered something for Sienna here without asking her, so if she wants something else..."

Sienna shook her head.

"We're ordering pizza. What kind do you want?" Leland asked.

"I don't want any," Earl said.

"Famous last words. I'll get you pepperoni— your favorite. What about your friend?"

"Anything is fine," Sienna said.

"Okay," Leland said. "What do you need?"

"Encrypted USB. We want to know what's inside."

"When do you need it?"

"Tonight."

Leland laughed. "We're swamped tonight. How about tomorrow?"

"No. Sorry. We need help now," Earl said.

"When can you get the USB over here?"

"We're five minutes from your office."

"No kidding. You're practically knocking on my front door, huh?" Leland laughed.

"One more thing." Earl glanced at Sienna.

"Nope." And Leland hung up.

Earl drew a deep breath. "She's never been rude to me. Must have a lot on her plate."

"You must know her well if you're making excuses for her," Sienna said.

"Well, I've worked with her before. We all have. She's the go-to tech person whenever Hu Knows needs something." Earl pulled into the parking lot of a large office complex. "We're here, but give me a second. I need to make a call."

Sienna nodded. What else could she do? She had no idea where they were.

Earl parked the car and called Deshon. "Everything okay?"

Listening, he nodded a few times. "Good. Keep my SUV there for the weekend."

Sienna could not hear the other end of the conversation.

"Yes, there's one more thing. This afternoon, a woman by the name of Dana Nesbitt was shot in her home." Earl gave Deshon the home address. "She was transported to Grady. Could you please find out what her status is?"

Sienna sniffled. She quickly prayed for Dana, that God would heal her and not let any harm befall the baby in her womb.

"I know, right? I never imagined being an accountant could be deadly," Earl said on the phone. "No need. Just text me as soon as you find something. Yeah. Okay. Thanks, man."

After he hung up, Earl turned to Sienna. "Deshon is going to let us know about Dana's status. He's heading to the hospital."

"Thank you." And she meant it.

CHAPTER EIGHT

"A whistle from the whistleblower." Cayson Yang studied the whistle USB that Sienna had handed over to him. He spun around in his ergonomic chair.

Earl sat next to him in another chair, but Sienna chose to stand as she ate her stir-fried shrimp noodles right out of the box using a pair of chopsticks. Earl had offered her his seat earlier. He had found a big chair to sit in so that he could share it with his messenger bag. The strap was still around his shoulder.

As for dinner, Earl had gulped down his chicken lettuce wrap quickly, tossed out the containers, washed his hands, and sat back down next to Cayson, who barely started on the whistle. Sometimes his colleagues said he ate too fast.

"You don't find it funny?" Cayson's eyebrows rose. He glanced over at his cousin as if to get support. Leland Yang-Joule waved him off.

"Find what funny?" Earl shook his head.

"I said this is a whistle from the whistleblower," Cayson repeated.

When no one reacted, Cayson brushed them off. "Never mind."

There were other people in the machine room, but they didn't talk to Earl or Sienna. They were in the middle of some project that Earl wasn't privy to.

"Should we wait here and watch you crack open that USB drive?" Earl asked.

Before Cayson could answer, the door opened and in walked BBI Special Agent Stella Evans with a stack of pizzas.

"Stella," Earl said. He knew immediately that the project was related to the federal government.

Sienna looked surprised that Earl had called the agent by her first name. Earl didn't feel the need to explain. Maybe later. Or not.

Stella ignored Earl. She turned to Sienna. "You must be Sienna. You didn't specify a topping, so just take whatever you want."

"Thanks," Sienna said.

"That smells good," Earl said. "How are you and your partner doing?"

Stella put down the pizza boxes on an empty table near a coffee maker. "Jake's over the moon. His wife is due in a few weeks."

"Already?" Earl remembered when he had accompanied FBI Special Agent Jake Kessler to California a few years before to hunt down clues to the lost Amber Room. Stella wasn't directly involved, but Earl had met her later. They had gone out exactly once, but Stella allowed him to call her by her first name.

Earl figured he probably needed to stop going out with every woman he met on the job.

"I know, right? It has been a few years since they got married," Stella said.

"I got it started," Cayson announced. "But this is military grade encryption worthy of NSA."

"Meaning?" Earl asked.

"Meaning it's going to take a while," Cayson replied. "Who encrypted this?"

Earl looked at Sienna.

"I don't know," she said.

"You went to Arun." Earl kept his voice low so that he didn't scare Sienna. He was still getting to know her and wasn't sure what she could or could not handle. "Do you think your Printer Guy might know?"

Sienna drew a deep breath. "I was hoping that Arun could read it for me, but he got miffed and asked why Dana gave it to me."

"So he knew that the whistle came from Dana."

"Sounds like it." Sienna didn't say more.

Perhaps there was nothing more to say. The smell of pizza distracted him.

Stella placed two slices of pepperoni on a paper plate and handed it to Earl. "I knew your lettuce wrap was just an appetizer."

Earl shrugged.

"How does she know what you ordered?" Sienna asked.

"Well, she's FBI. She knows everything," Cayson said. "Having dated each other also helps."

Earl watched Sienna's face. Was she jealous at all? He couldn't detect anything of that sort, but he kept staring because there was something about Sienna. In spite of the pain and pressure, she still appeared calm. Perhaps she had a natural poker face. If so, what was she thinking? What was she hiding?

She had been forthcoming on the drive here, but there was still a whole lot more Earl needed to know. What could Sienna tell him about Zachary Gavard?

Earl's phone buzzed. He read the text message from Deshon. He called him back. "What?"

"Texted you."

"I know. I couldn't believe it. If the ambulance didn't get to Grady, where did it go?" Earl asked.

"I called Helen, but she said it will be a while. She left a message for Leland."

"Leland?" If Helen needed Leland, then it was all above their pay grades. "I'm in Leland's office building. I'll ask her myself."

"About your SUV," Deshon said. "There are two sets of bugs and one tracker. Plus cameras everywhere. How did they get inside your vehicle?"

"I gave Agent Kimball my key fob outside Dana's house so she could move it for me."

"Makes sense then. There was another tracker under the SUV. A classic piece. That one might not be FBI."

"No fingerprints, of course."

"No. And no way to trace back to whoever did it. It was encrypted."

"Ah, that word again. No idea when it was planted?" Earl asked.

"No way to know."

"Thanks, Deshon. Good job."

"No problem. I'm going home now to get some shut-eye. Anything else you need?" Deshon asked.

"I think that's all for now." After Earl hung up, he realized that all eyes were on him.

"What about Leland?" Cayson asked, nibbling the crust of his pizza. "I heard you mention her name."

"My associate is unable to find out where Dana has been taken," Earl said. "She has a gunshot wound. And she's visibly pregnant. Kimball said they were taking her to Grady. She never showed."

"Kimball?" Stella asked.

"Agent Mariana Kimball. You know her?"

Stella shook her head. "I can find out."

"Kimball or someone called the ambulance— that's my guess," Earl said. "Now Dana has disappeared."

"Or in another hospital," Stella said. "If you can tell me more, I'll find out for you."

Earl almost forgot about Sienna standing there. She was frozen in place. As Earl summarized for Stella, he reached out for Sienna's hand. She let him hold it.

A smile escaped Stella's mouth. "You two together?"

Sienna dropped Earl's hand.

"We're pretending," Earl said.

"Some acting there. I couldn't tell." Stella swiped her phone. "Let me see what's going on."

Sienna glanced at Earl. "Agent Kimball…"

Earl nodded. "Stella, could you ask without Kimball knowing? We don't know if we can trust her. Perez, you know."

"I got that." Stella frowned, as if she didn't like being told what to do.

"I wasn't trying to tell you what to do. I was just reminding you, that's all."

Stella continued frowning. "That's why it didn't work out between us."

Earl dared not look at Sienna. He didn't want to know her reaction.

While Stella was on the phone, Earl called Helen. Before he could say anything, she switched to video.

"Arun Dhillon." Helen's hair was wrapped in a towel and she was sitting on her balcony in Santorini. Behind her was the blue morning sky and the Aegean Sea.

"How did you know?" Earl asked.

"I'm ahead of you." Helen smiled. "He used to work for the Indian military. Left for a cushy job in the corporate world to appease his girlfriend, who was scared he'd die in the military. Soon after, she dumped him and married his best friend."

"Ouch."

"With a H-1B visa, Arun came to the USA. He's in his fourth of six years here."

Earl nodded. "Somehow he ended up fixing printers for GOOP?"

"He did that and more for Gavard."

"Mr. Ford, you mean."

"No, Zachary Gavard," Helen repeated. "He had Arun's private phone number that no one else in the company had."

Interesting. So far they had focused on Finnegan Ford, the CEO of GOOP. The shadow in the dark might just be Zachary Gavard.

"I'll send you more information as it comes in," Helen said.

"Thank you." Earl hung up. He was about to tell Sienna something when he caught the tail end of her conversation with Stella.

"That can't be. She was injured and pregnant." Sienna turned to Earl. "The ambulance never went to Grady's, unlike what Agent Kimball said. This confirms what Deshon told us—that no one by the name Dana was in the hospital."

"They can still treat her somewhere else," Stella replied.

"Like where? Another hospital?" Sienna asked.

"Weird." Earl waited for Stella to tell him more.

He recalled asking Kimball about it on his drive from Conyers. "Why would Agent Kimball lie to us?"

"I can't tell you much more," Stella said. "All I can say is that the US Marshals got involved. You know what that means."

"Can you tell me if she's safe though?" Earl asked.

Stella barely nodded.

That told Earl everything. Dana might be in protective custody or she might be in WITSEC. If so, then was the shooting at her kitchen window staged?

"I don't understand," Sienna said. "Where is Dana?"

"My guess is she's in WITSEC," Earl said to her. Stella didn't refute him.

"WITSEC?" Sienna said. "That means she helped the FBI then?"

Earl nodded. "And that her life was in danger."

"Have they identified the second attacker?" Earl asked Stella.

"I have no idea, but he is dead." Stella picked up another piece of pizza. "I think you need to talk to Agent Kimball."

"Do you trust her?"

"I think so."

Earl nodded. "Okay. I take your word for it. Thank you."

"Don't mention it." Stella sat down on the other side of Cayson.

There was nothing Earl could do. If Stella was untrustworthy, she'd probably tell Agent Kimball where they were. "About Agent Kimball, could you hold off telling her where we are right now?"

"Sure. I'm not involved," Stella said.

"Remember three years ago, there was a mole in the FBI?" Earl asked.

"Yeah."

"Well, the bureau might not be totally sanitized yet."

"Oh?" Stella did not look surprised.

"You knew."

Stella didn't reply.

"Be careful," Earl said.

Stella nodded.

Earl stood up and stretched. "I need to get some sleep. Is the lounge available?"

"Sure," Cayson said. "You know where everything is."

"Thanks."

To Sienna, Earl said, "There's a kitchen there and some seats where you can catch a nap."

"No. I have to stay with the whistle," Sienna replied. Her voice was cracking.

"Are you okay?" Earl reached for her.

Sienna wiped her eyes. "I'm glad Dana is in WITSEC. For her sake and her baby's."

"We'll get to the bottom of this." Earl gently wiped a tear from her cheek.

Sienna nodded.

CHAPTER NINE

Bones aching, Earl dragged himself down the hallway toward the lounge. He made it there just as Leland was making coffee in the break room that took up a third of the area. The rest of the space was filled with chaise lounge chairs, hammocks, sofas, and recliners.

"Want some Kona?" Leland asked.

"Not right now. Thanks. I need to get some sleep." However, Earl walked into the break room toward Leland instead of to the lounge area. "May I ask you something?"

"Anything for Helen." Leland washed a couple of mugs that had been left on the countertop near the kitchen sink.

Here was one of the world's most formidable

hackers, washing mugs by hand. Leland's humility and helpful spirit were why Earl respected her.

"I don't want to take advantage of you," Earl said.

"But."

"Someone wants to kill my whistleblower, but we don't know who the enemy is," Earl said.

"Go on."

"This afternoon, we went to see her friend—who was fired from the company. She got shot while standing at the kitchen sink. She's pregnant. The FBI came, and so did the ambulance. She was alive when we left her—according to Agent Kimball, who also told us they were taking her to Grady. However, Deshon went to the hospital and Dana never arrived. Helen told Deshon that we have no access to hospitals. Stella called around but she couldn't tell us anything."

"You're telling me that because you know I love a mystery." Leland dried the mugs.

"There's more. When we got to the safe house, someone had killed Agent Perez and taken her place. We escaped—long story—and then I found out that my SUV was bugged by two different entities. So we took another car here. And the FBI is already here."

"Stella?" Leland asked.

"I don't know what to think."

"Stella is here to observe Cayson's project. I'm actually leaving in twenty-four hours for another project." Leland poured coffee into a clean mug. "You sure you don't want any coffee? This is the best."

Earl shook his head. "Twenty-four hours."

"Enough time to do something." Leland sipped coffee. "Is that what you're asking me?"

"I've owed you so much."

"Someday I'll call for help and you'll come running, right?"

"Absolutely."

"What do you need?"

"Are you sure? It might cross the line."

"I'll knock. If the door doesn't open, there's nothing I can do."

"Fair enough." Earl glanced this way and that. They were the only people in the break room. "I need to know whether Dana Nesbitt is alive and if her unborn baby is okay."

"Logically, if the FBI did not follow through with the missing ambulance, what's the first thing that pops into your mind?" Leland asked.

"WITSEC."

"Then we'll start from there. Give me everything you have. Dana's home address, contact information, anything."

Earl realized his phone was still in his SUV. His burner phone was of no help. However, he still had his laptop inside his messenger bag, which never left his shoulder. At the kitchen counter, he booted up his laptop and gave Leland all the information she needed.

Leland pointed to the clock on the wall. It was almost one in the morning. "When do you need the information?"

"Sienna and I are supposed to fly out to Savannah at eight o'clock in the morning for a conference," Earl said. "It's possible that the FBI would be waiting at the airport for us."

"Are you harboring a fugitive?"

"Sienna is not one."

"Is the FBI coming after you?"

"They weren't. Now I don't know. On the one hand, Agent Kimball is supposed to be on our side. On the other hand, they were infiltrated by a fake Agent Perez."

"Why don't you drive to Savannah? It's only five hours."

"I drove from there to here yesterday. However, Sienna's boss is on the flight. We don't want him to be suspicious."

"Earl."

"What?"

"I'm sure he's already suspicious—if not of your girlfriend, but of an ex-employee such as Dana, right?" Leland drank her coffee.

"I'm glad I talked with you. You helped me clear my thoughts," Earl said.

"If you had gotten enough sleep, you'd have come to the same conclusions."

"Would I?"

"Wouldn't you?" Leland asked. "Let me see what I can do about the information you seek."

"Please don't tell Stella or anyone in the FBI."

"Just stay alive, Earl."

"I try my best. I want to hug you but it might not be appropriate."

"Is it? So hug me, man. It's not like we're an item or anything." Leland put down her coffee mug.

"That will get me in trouble with Dario." Earl laughed.

"Dario?" Leland's eyes widened.

"He's got a thing for you." Earl gave her a big-brother bear hug.

"Does he?" Leland sounded perplexed. "How do you know?"

"I know men."

"Remind me to ask for relationship advice from someone who can't hang on to a girlfriend for more than a couple of months." Leland returned to her cup of coffee.

Earl laughed. "That's because I knew they wouldn't work out. I'm going to know when I meet the one. I'll know right away or soon enough."

Leland didn't reply.

Earl glanced over his shoulder. Sienna walked past the break room door.

"When do you think you might have something?" Earl asked.

"Depends on what I can find."

"Great. Thanks." Earl rushed toward Sienna, who was sitting down on one of the sofas. She kicked off her shoes and lay down.

"Are you okay?" Earl asked, kneeling at the sofa so that he was at eye level with Sienna.

"I have a bad headache." Sienna's voice was low. "Do you have Tylenol or something?"

"I'll see what I can find." Earl caught Leland before she left the area.

A couple of minutes later, he returned with a bottled water and two tablets, only to find Sienna softly sobbing.

Earl gently helped her sit up. He sat down next to her.

"Thank you." After Sienna drank the water, she said, "I have a feeling that Dana is dead. Another fake agent got her. Maybe even the same fake Perez."

"We don't know."

"That's our problem, isn't it? We don't know anything." Sienna made a fist and pounded Earl's thigh. "Oh sorry. I didn't mean to take it out on you."

Earl wrapped his hand over Sienna's fist and held it on his thigh.

"We had a long day and now it looks like we might have a long night too," Earl said. "Shall we pray for God's peace and help?"

"Please." Sienna curled up her legs and closed her eyes.

Before Earl finished his prayer, Sienna had fallen asleep against his arm. He gently put her down on the sofa. He found a cushion to prop up her head. And a soft throw to cover the rest of her.

Sitting on the other end of the sofa, Earl finished praying in silence, asking God for wisdom and direction.

He couldn't sleep.

He thought of Leland's coffee. He went to the break room and took the entire carafe with him, together with the largest mug he could find on the shelf.

He walked back down the hallway. Entering the workroom, he saw Stella, Cayson, and other Binary Systems employees in a meeting behind a glass door. It was almost two o'clock in the morning. It seemed that the company never slept.

Leland was at her workstation. She waved to him. "Got something here."

Earl grabbed a nearby chair and sat down. "What did you find?"

"What we suspected. Dana Nesbitt is in WITSEC. The US Marshals took over once the ambulance was delivered." Leland pointed to the street cam outside Atlanta.

"You traced the ambulance all the way to Newnan?"

"Yep."

"She's alive."

"As far as I can tell. That was a cruel plan if it was a ruse."

"Cruel? How?" Leland asked. "Keeps Dana and her baby alive."

"Made Sienna sad."

Leland smiled. "You care for her."

"Sure. I care for everyone I work with, including you."

"Not the same way you care for her. I can see it in your face."

"Come on." Earl laughed.

"You don't believe in love at first sight?" Leland chuckled.

"Not at all."

Before Leland could ask him any more questions, Cayson and Stella came out of their meeting.

Earl followed Cayson back to his workstation. "Anything yet?"

"Nothing." Cayson sat down. "You might want to get some sleep. Keep an eye on your girlfriend so she doesn't run off again."

"How did you know she ran?" Earl asked.

"I told him." Stella walked toward them with a mug of coffee in her hand. "Word gets around. Every agent has been informed that you two have gone dark."

"Something was off about the safe house operation."

"You don't trust Kimball."

"Sienna doesn't trust her."

"You have no opinion."

"I have no idea who to believe. I trust you, and you say?" Earl asked.

"I say that you need to trust Agent Kimball. No matter how it looks." Stella sipped coffee.

No matter how it looks? "What does that mean?"

"Remember our friend Jake?"

Earl nodded. FBI Special Agent Jake Kessler was in deep undercover for three years chasing down the world's most notorious terrorist, Molyneux.

In fact, her web was so far-reaching that every agency was still dealing with the fallout. Of course, Jake became a hero, although he moved to another entity. Now he was chasing after cybercriminals, as Stella was.

"Hey, thanks for taking time out of your schedule to help us," Earl said to her.

"You happened to show up at the right time," Stella said. "We have a lull in our project right now. Besides, I'm just an observer this time, and I need something to do. Anything else I can help you with while I watch Cayson work?"

Cayson chuckled. "What? You don't like to watch me work?"

Stella grinned. "I'd rather watch paint dry, but the FBI wants to make sure that our interests are protected."

"This network is in Europe," Cayson said. "Oops. I said too much already."

"You can trust Earl. We all do," Stella said. "The question is whether Sienna trusts you, Earl."

"I don't know if she does." Earl thought he and Sienna were getting along well enough, but beyond that, he wasn't entirely sure. "I suspect there are still things that she hasn't told Helen when they talked, and hasn't told me on the drive here."

"What exactly has she done?" Stella asked.

"She was telling on her boss, and if he finds out she has contacted the FBI about the embezzlements and shell companies, what do you think he might do to her to save his job and reputation?" Earl asked.

"If she no longer trusts Kimball, then she might feel that her whistleblowing is backfiring."

"Who else can she turn to?"

"I don't know how you can get her to trust you right away," Stella said.

"I told her to trust God for me."

"Good advice. Meanwhile, let me dig around and see if I can assist in some way."

"Thank you, Stella." Earl fist-bumped with Stella and then made his way back to the lounge, praying for ways to get Sienna to trust him.

He recalled what Sienna had told him on the drive from Conyers.

I'm afraid of what might happen to me, to my family.

If her family was safe, then Sienna would worry less, right?

In the lounge, Sienna was still sleeping on the sofa. She looked peaceful but tired.

Earl sat across from her, and logged in to his laptop. He chatted with a security company that sometimes did work for Hu Knows, Inc., and asked for personnel to keep an eye on Uncle Tabbebo and Sienna's mom in Chattanooga.

When they named their daily rate, Earl almost whistled. The price had gone up. Helen would hit the ceiling when she saw the bill.

But what is the price of life?

Across the coffee table between the two sofas, Sienna's eyes opened.

"Has Cayson found anything?" she asked.

Earl shook his head. "Not yet, but he's working on it."

"We must go to the conference," Sienna said. "Mr. Ford will think something is wrong if I don't show up. If I can get him to say something that the FBI can use against him, then my job is done."

"Dana was shot. Arun is dead. Your old boyfriend Rocco is also dead. You might be next."

Earl wasn't trying to scare her, but facts didn't change.

"I don't trust the FBI anymore if they let a fake agent infiltrate their ranks."

"The FBI I know is better trained than that," Earl said. "I wonder if they let her in for a reason."

"What would be the reason?" Sienna brushed her hair with her fingers. "They said they would protect me, but they let that man point a gun at me in Dana's house, remember?"

"Thank God you're okay."

"If you hadn't gotten there in time..." Her voice trailed off.

Suddenly Sienna sat up, bed head and all. Her eyes widened. "My mom and uncle."

"Taken care of," Earl said calmly. For once, he was ahead of Sienna—by a few minutes.

"What?"

"I just talked to some associates of ours. They're on their way to Chattanooga as we speak."

"What time is it?"

"Uh, just a few minutes after three."

"Only? I thought I slept all night."

"It's going to be a long night, so go back to sleep. I'll let you know when Cayson finds something."

"What if we miss our flight?"

"From the looks of it, we'll most certainly miss

our flight." Earl closed his laptop. He dug into his messenger bag for a power cord, and plugged in his laptop. "You'll need to come up with an excuse why you're not on the same flight as Mr. Ford."

"If I say I overslept, he will know it's a lie. I never oversleep."

"No?" Earl laughed. "I oversleep all the time."

"By now he will know that Dana is in hiding and Arun is dead. He'll be suspicious if I don't show up at the airport."

"I don't want you to be in a public place for a while. I can't protect you at the airport," Earl said.

"You were okay flying with me."

"That was before Arun blew up in his van. Now I'm trying to figure out how to keep you safe. I'm not sure we should even be at the resort."

"It's my last chance to record Mr. Ford. He's going to let his guard down at Moss Grand Bahama. There will be other billionaires there, and he might even find a new girlfriend. He might be intoxicated and he's going to talk."

"A lot of 'mights' there."

"Keep me safe, Mr. Young. That's what my uncle paid you for."

CHAPTER TEN

S ienna woke up at nine thirty, more than an hour after her flight left Atlanta. She wanted to scream, but no sound came from her mouth. This was the first time in a long time that she had been late for anything at work. She was sure she had set her alarm—

No, she hadn't.

She didn't have her phone with her. Earl's friend had taken it when he hauled his SUV away.

She stared at the ceiling, remembered where she was. Then she closed her eyes.

The job was hers to lose, and she probably had.

"Lord Jesus, I have to trust that You are working this out for my good." Her whispered prayer was interrupted by the smell of coffee wafting over her nose.

She opened one eye.

Earl placed a mug on the coffee table next to Sienna's sofa. "Kona with a light shot of milk."

"How did you know?"

"Profile."

"Ah, yes. I forgot," Sienna said. "You didn't wake me up. We missed the flight."

"I just got up myself." Earl sat down on a nearby armchair. "We'll have to come up with an excuse to take a later flight. The good news is that there are several flights to Freeport this weekend. The other good news is that your conference doesn't start until Monday."

"Everyone from GOOP will be there by today or tomorrow. Ford, Gavard, his wife, plus the board, and their investors," Sienna said. "If I'm missing, they'll ask questions."

"Let's see what the agenda is." Earl scrolled down his phone. "Opening remarks by Finnegan Ford, and keynote by Zachary Gavard."

"I'll be working, so I'll be with Mr. Ford all week," Sienna said. "Maybe he'll say something to me about Dana."

"I can't be with you at work all day long," Earl said.

"Yeah, that would be awkward. I'll be with Mr. Ford, probably in meeting rooms and at conferences."

"However, I can put a tracker on you." Earl produced a watch. "I just got this from Cayson. It's top of the line. Never take it off."

Sienna stretched out her left wrist so that Earl could put the watch on.

"It's waterproof and actually tells time." Earl smiled.

"But I can take it off."

"Sure."

Sienna took off the watch just to be sure she could. She put it back on again. "Thank you. I'd hate it if I can't take it off."

"Like an ankle monitor?"

"I wouldn't know." Sienna stared at the watch. It had a stainless steel band and a digital clock face. It wasn't what she would have bought at the jeweler's. "Couldn't you just watch me through the security cameras?"

Earl shook his head. "When I contacted Moss Grand Bahama security, I found out they're working with the FBI and the local police. I'm going to get a tour because I know the Chief of Security, but I don't know if they'll let me in the rest of the time."

"You can play the role of the ultra-worried, paranoid boyfriend."

"You betcha. At other times, I'll hang out by the pool and mingle with their significant others."

"Sounds like a plan."

Earl pointed in the direction of a nearby hallway. "Disposable toothbrush and toothpaste kits are in the locker room, together with clean towels and soap for a shower if you need."

"My clothes are in the safe house."

"So are mine, but I have some spare shirts and shorts in my backpack. You can wear them if you want." Earl sipped his coffee. Steam rose in front of his face. "We'll shop via VPN as soon as we want, and we'll send someone to do curbside pickup for us."

Slowly, Sienna sat up. She massaged her neck. There was a kink there. "Maybe I pulled a muscle."

"Or maybe it's just stress. Would you like me to... Uh, never mind."

"Normally, no. But since you're supposed to be my boyfriend, why not?"

"I learned a few things in the Army." Earl put down his coffee mug.

"First, let me brush my teeth so I can drink my coffee while it's hot." Sienna got up and walked to the locker room.

She returned a few minutes later to find Earl standing behind the sofa, waiting for her to sit down.

"You're serious about it, aren't you?" Sienna asked.

"Yep. Your neck will feel much better after this." Earl rubbed his palms together to warm them up. "Where does it hurt?"

"Here." Sienna pointed to the side of her neck. "And here."

She sat there patiently as Earl massaged her neck up to the base of her head. She closed her eyes and enjoyed the warmth of his hands.

A sliding door opened and Cayson Yang rushed in. His hair was askew and his tee shirt had what looked like coffee stain in the front of it. His flip-flops slapped the wood floor as he made his way to Sienna and Earl.

"Whassup?" Earl continued to massage Sienna's neck. "Any news for us about the USB drive?"

"Not yet." Cayson placed his tablet on the table in front of Sienna. "First, very bad news. Your boss is dead."

"What?" Sienna brushed Earl's hands off her shoulder. "What did you say?"

Earl came around and sat on the sofa next to Sienna.

Cayson tapped Play on the video. On the screen, a reporter at the Miami International Airport was talking into the camera. Cayson rewound the video to the beginning.

"Breaking news at the Miami International Airport," the reporter said. "A man has died onboard an Air Tropical Airline flight from Atlanta to Miami en route to Freeport in the Bahamas. Witnesses said they thought the man was taking a nap in his first-class seat on the two-hour flight. However, when the time came for them to put their seats upright, his girlfriend and the flight attendants discovered that the man had passed away."

"Do we know who he is?" the newscaster asked.

"Yes. His girlfriend, Genevieve Reid, identified him as billionaire Finnegan Ford, CEO and co-founder of Gavard Owens Oppenheimer Properties, Inc., a real estate investment firm based out of Atlanta."

"A co-founder? His name is not on the company name."

"That's observant of you, Sally," the reporter said. "I don't know why his name is not on there."

"What do we know about Mr. Ford?"

"He leaves behind two daughters by his ex-wife. His girlfriend is not taking any questions."

"Thank you, Amelia. That's Amelia Soto

reporting from the Miami International Airport," the newscaster said. "We will bring you more news when it's available."

Cayson stopped the video. "That was a good question. Why isn't Ford's name on the company name?"

"Word around the water cooler said that it would have spelled GOOF," Sienna replied. "The investors decided to salvage their acronym by replacing Ford with Properties."

No one laughed.

Sienna kept her breathing steady. "I can't believe it."

Earl called Helen, who was monitoring intel for him and Sienna. Helen didn't answer the phone. Earl left her a message.

Cayson waved to Agent Stella Evans as she walked through the door. "She knows."

Stella stood by the sofa. Her hands were in her pant pockets. "You told her?"

"I showed them the local news from Miami."

Stella turned to Sienna. "No word yet whether there was foul play, but the passenger manifest says Finnegan Ford and Genevieve Reid were onboard. I called the FBI office in Miami, and they confirmed it's him at the coroner's."

Sienna gasped.

"I'll keep you posted on the investigation." Stella sighed. "Was he really only fifty-five?"

Sienna nodded. "He's very healthy, and has no vices except for wine and women."

Earl cleared his throat. He was too far away to hold her hand. "You okay?"

"No, I'm not okay," Sienna said. "That's three people from GOOP dead in one year. Anyone know what's going on?"

"The GBI and FBI are working on it," Stella said. "Since Mr. Ford died in Florida airspace, the FBI wants to know if it's of natural causes or foul play."

Sienna could only hope that the Georgia Bureau of Investigations, along with their federal counterparts, would scour the company top down. There were so many things wrong with GOOP, from hiring and firing practices to the various trans-actions under the table.

"They would want to talk to me," Sienna said. "At this moment, I'm missing."

"You were supposed to be on the flight," Stella said.

"Yes, sitting next to Earl in business class." Someone else came to Sienna's mind. "Is Agent Kimball involved?"

"You mean in the investigation or as a suspect?"
Stella laughed.

Earl did not laugh. "What do you advise, Stella?"

Stella still did not sit down. "It's problematic
that you and Sienna fled the safe house. And then
fled the Conyers crime scene. And then didn't show
up at the safe house or airport."

"You're saying we look suspicious," Sienna said.

"Don't you?" Stella asked.

"Well, you might have a point," Earl said.
"Three people have died—and two within twelve
hours of each other. One is in WITSEC. On top of
that, the safe house was compromised. It can be
said that we don't trust the FBI—with the exception
of you—at this time."

"By not disclosing that I know where you two
are, I've allowed you two to put me in a bad position," Stella said.

Sienna listened and agreed. She didn't want
Stella to tell the FBI where she was. Not just yet.
Not when there were bad apples in the bureau.

And not when there was something she had to
do. If Mr. Ford was really dead, then she had to
carry out the instructions he had given her several
months back after it had been confirmed that Rocco
was murdered. Sienna wasn't sure why Mr. Ford

had trusted her so much. Perhaps her loyalty and the fact that she answered to God might have swayed his judgement of her.

"I have an out for you." Earl leaned back against the sofa. "You can start looking into Agent Kimball. Something is off. She said Dana was at Grady, and then we found out she didn't go there. She's in WITSEC. Kimball is my handler, and yet the safe house was so insecure that Killjoy Burditt found it, killed Agent Perez, and took her place before anyone realized it."

"And she let you play a role in the operation." Cayson pointed to Earl. "You're a civilian."

"On the contrary, my being a civilian is an advantage," Earl said. "I'm not an undercover agent. At Hu Knows, I'm already under the radar, so they won't find my employment records anywhere. I'm perpetually in between jobs."

"I can't believe Mr. Ford is dead." Sienna held back her tears. "Then it's over—all this to-do that I have with the FBI. How could anyone testify against a dead man?"

"Well, he might have accomplices."

"To be honest with you, I still don't believe that Mr. Ford embezzled company funds. I was shocked when I discovered the transactions, but even that was something I stumbled on," Sienna explained. "I was having lunch with Dana at her desk while she was working and it was on her screen."

"Did she mean to show you deliberately?" Earl asked.

"That's an interesting question." Sienna wondered about that angle which she hadn't thought of before. "What do you mean, exactly?"

"I'm sure the FBI is exploring all angles. I was only wondering if Mr. Ford was set up. Now that he's dead, he can't defend himself."

Stella nodded. "Good point. Let's say that Mr. Ford might not be the only person interested in siphoning off billions of dollars from GOOP."

Cayson laughed. "Why on earth is it GOOP? They could have rearranged it to say POGO or something else."

Sienna shrugged. "I wasn't there when Gavard and Mr. Ford started the company with their inheritance money after their mother passed away. She handed them some old money, and the two of them multiplied it into billions with savvy investments. Word was, they both had a keen sense of where they should put their money."

"They mostly buy commercial buildings, yes?" Earl asked. "And land. I remember that much from what Helen sent me."

"GOOP buys and sells anything you can claim

as real estate," Sienna said for the benefit of Stella and Cayson. "Lately, they have sold a tremendous amount of land and buildings to people outside the USA. Unlike other countries, ours doesn't have a rule that says you can't sell to foreign interests."

"And that's where the FBI comes in," Earl added. "Some of the sales are to shell companies or to government entities that aren't friends of the USA."

Sienna had nothing verifiable to say. Dana, Rocco, and Arun had been snooping around. "I just work there. They pay me a salary, plus Christmas bonuses—which I'm assuming I'm not getting now. All I know is that we have dead employees, plus an accountant in WITSEC."

Stella shifted on her feet. "You called the FBI, though."

"Because I saw things I probably shouldn't have, and after I did, I felt threatened at work." Sienna regretted seeing what had been on Dana's computer screen. "I didn't call the FBI until after Rocco was murdered."

She wondered if she should start looking for a new job. But she had made a promise to Mr. Ford that if he died—especially suddenly—that she would do this one thing for him. Now that made her wonder if she had wronged Mr. Ford by talking to the FBI.

"What if Mr. Ford was set up and I played right into it?" Sienna asked.

"Did you just call the FBI hotline?" Stella seemed to be still asking about the whistleblowing.

"No. Dana gave me Agent Kimball's name. In fact, Kimball was the same contact for Rocco." It was starting to make sense.

A movement made Sienna look up. She glanced over at Cayson, who had to leave.

"And Arun?" Earl asked. "Was Arun a whistle-blower too?"

"I have no idea." Sienna looked at Stella.

"I'll find out." The FBI agent made a note on her phone as she followed Cayson. "All right. I better get back to the machine room. I'm supposed to shadow Cayson. See? He's gone."

CHAPTER ELEVEN

When they were alone again, Sienna and Earl looked at each other.

"Do you think someone killed Mr. Ford?" Sienna asked.

"If someone did, then your life is in graver danger than we thought."

"What should I do?"

"I don't think you can go to the conference now."

"I'm sure it'll be canceled. I need to log in to my work computer." Sienna eyed Earl's laptop which he had left on the coffee table while it was being charged the night before.

"Let me ask Cayson to give you a secure laptop." Earl got up from the sofa. "More coffee?"

Sienna peeked into her coffee mug. She could see the bottom. "Did I drink all that?"

"While we were conversing. It was probably automatic." Earl chuckled.

"Probably. Well, I don't need more coffee. I found the women's locker room. Did you say you have a spare shirt and a pair of shorts?"

Earl nodded. He retrieved his backpack from near the sofa. "Black or gray?"

"Gray."

Earl tossed her the tee shirt. It was crumpled, but smelled of fabric softener.

"Gym shorts or cycling shorts?" Earl lifted them.

The gym shorts looked too large for her, but the bike shorts looked like they were made of spandex. They would be snug on Earl, but probably loose on her. She pointed to the bright tangerine cycling shorts.

"Good choice. It's stretchable." He tossed her the pair of shorts.

"I'll be right back." Sienna headed for the shower.

"Meanwhile, I'll ask Cayson for a spare laptop —or two for both of us."

"Thank you. You're so sweet."

"I wanted to say I get paid to do this, but even if I wasn't, I'd still do it," Earl said.

It was touching. "I appreciate it. Hopefully, it will be over soon and we can get back to our own lives."

"You know, I kind of like our friendship."

"Without the deaths around us," Sienna said quietly.

"Right." Earl sighed. "If we didn't have any of these dark things happening, and we somehow met, would you have gone out with me for coffee or something?"

"If we lived in the same city, sure." Sienna meant it. "Considering we both know Helen and could have met through her, I don't see why we couldn't have coffee."

"Or lunch."

"Yeah. Why not?"

They stood there, wordlessly.

Sienna broke the impasse. "Would you please tell Cayson I want a light laptop?"

"Yes. I'll do that." Earl drew a deep breath.

Sienna had no idea what was on his mind, but something had changed between them. They had been with each other twenty-four seven since Thursday, and had known each other for one week since he arrived from Savannah for their "dress rehearsal."

Whatever it was, she felt that they had built a rapport, in spite of the dire circumstances in which they had found themselves. They were both still alive, and had survived Dana's house, Kimball's safe house, and Arun's house.

God had protected both of them.

For a reason.

Sienna found a shower kit in the bathroom. It had a clean towel, a hand towel, and a face towel in it, together with a new bar of soap, hotel-size bottles of shampoo and conditioner, and a thin pair of disposable sandals for the shower stall.

Someone had thought about all that.

The water pressure was excellent and the rain shower was a luxury. Sienna figured Binary Systems employees practically lived in the building. That explained the lounge area looking like a sprawling day hotel at some airports in the world, next to a full-size kitchen, where employees could cook meals—if they had time at all.

Standing under the pulsating streams of warm water, Sienna could not see her way through the mess she was in. GOOP was living up to its name, after all.

What had they wanted from Rocco? Arun? Mr. Ford?

Or had it all been a great big lie? Were they really dead? Sienna hadn't seen any of their bodies. Where was the proof?

Perhaps they were all alive somewhere in the world, away from the woes of working at a multi-billion-dollar venture capitalist firm that probably had more enemies than friends. At least, Mr. Ford had told her so.

He had said many things to her in the privacy of his office that she could not tell anyone else. Granted, there were things she would never say to anyone because they pertained to his estranged wife before their messy divorce.

Interestingly, Melissa Ford had zero interest in her then-husband's company. She had focused on raising her two daughters, who would rather be social-media influencers than go to business school like their dad. After the divorce, she had sold her settlement shares to GOOP investors, and then moved the daughters home to Missouri.

That had been the last time Mr. Ford had spoken about his family. Shortly after the divorce, he started going out with his accountant—who was also Gavard's accountant.

Sienna wondered if Dana and Gavard could have...

Nah. Impossible. They disliked each other. Dana avoided talking to Gavard if at all possible—except at accounting meetings.

Sienna turned off the shower. In the changing zone, she found a hairdryer.

She still could not believe that Mr. Ford was dead. The embezzling investigation was still continuing. Would it ever get to court now?

To begin with, why would anyone accuse the soft-spoken Mr. Ford of embezzling money from his own company? While Gavard lived a lavish lifestyle with his superyacht on the Atlantic Ocean and his numerous vacation homes all over the world, Mr. Ford had been the opposite. Living frugally and driving his old Saab, he could have easily been mistaken for one of the executives rather than the CEO and part owner of the private company.

If anyone needed money, it would be Gavard.

However, how much did he want? With a personal fortune of at least fifty-billion dollars, Gavard could do anything he wanted.

His wife Celestia was one of the sweetest people Sienna had ever met. She was kind and generous, and still believed in sending handwritten Christmas cards year after year.

Sadly, the Gavards didn't have children of their own, and neither wanted to adopt—according to Dana, who was in the know. So there they were, in their late fifties, with no heirs to hand over their fortune to.

Earl's gray tee shirt was a hundred percent cotton. So soft and comfortable that Sienna could sleep in it. However, she couldn't. There was work to be done.

The shirt was long because Earl was tall. Sienna was pretty tall herself, at five foot nine, but his shirt still covered half her thighs, and therefore half of the tangerine shorts, which fitted her loosely.

By the time she came out of the locker room, Earl was sitting at a table with two laptops in front of him, and another guy, who was dressed in all black.

He didn't look up when Sienna approached them.

"Hey, you look great." Earl smiled. "I like my clothes on you...uh... That came out all wrong."

"I'll be sure to launder and fold them before I return them to you."

"I've set it up so the VPN comes on automatically," Computer Guy said. "Make sure that's the only route you take."

"Okay. What's my password again?" Earl wrote it down on a napkin.

"Don't write it down," Computer Guy said.

"How else am I going to remember it?" Earl grinned. "Sienna, this is Kelvin. He works in the computer room."

Kelvin waved without looking up. "Hey."

"Kelvin, this is Sienna," Earl said.

"I'll be done in a minute." Kelvin's eyes were on the laptop screen.

"When you're done, I need to talk with you," Sienna said to Earl.

Earl nodded. He seemed to be trying to read her expression.

Sienna kept a poker face. She didn't know who Kelvin was, and she wasn't about to say something he shouldn't hear.

Instead of waiting there, Sienna went to the kitchen to forage for breakfast. She found a box of smaller packets of oatmeal. Almost all of them had high sugar content and none of them were organic.

Then again, she might not live long enough to deal with the repercussions of the above.

She found a paper bowl, and heated the oatmeal in one of the two microwaves in the kitchen. While waiting for her oatmeal, she poured herself another cup of Kona black coffee.

She watched Kelvin walk out of the lounge.

Earl followed him but stopped at the kitchen. "You wanted to talk to me about something?"

"Is anyone else around?"

"All working." Earl poured himself another cup of coffee. "What is it about?"

Sienna kept her voice down. "You don't want me to run off and do my own thing."

"Uh-huh."

"I have to make a trip," Sienna said.

"What trip?"

"Side trip. I promised Mr. Ford that if he died suddenly, I'd do this for him."

"Do what?"

"You can't tell anyone."

Earl frowned. "Doesn't sound safe."

"I think he knew someone was coming after him. I felt bad when he told me that."

"Before or after you talked to the FBI?"

"After."

"Then I wonder if he was only trying to elicit sympathy out of you," Earl suggested.

"I've worked for him for ten years. I would've spotted it if he tried to manipulate my emotions."

"Would you? If you worked for him that long, could you have lost some perspective?"

"Well..." Sienna wasn't sure.

"Tell me I have a good point."

Sienna nodded. "Still, I promised him I'd do this one thing for him. I'm the only one who knows the combination of the—uh, never mind."

"Of a safe, perhaps?" Earl waited, as if he was the calmest person on earth. He drank coffee while he listened to Sienna.

"I'm not sure if I feel safe. I would feel better if you come with me."

"You know where we're going." More sips of coffee.

"Yes. I've been there before."

"And you want me to go with you."

"We might need your tow-truck friend if you can spare him."

"Because?" He put down the coffee mug.

"Because we could always use a third person."

"To?"

"To keep us safe." *When we get to the safe.*

"When do you need an answer?" Earl remained standing where he was by the counter, about four feet away from Sienna.

"Now."

"And when do we leave?"

"After we find out what's in the USB drive."

"That could be whenever."

"Then *whenever* it is," Sienna said. "I can't leave without the whistle."

She waited for Earl to respond. "Say something."

"Once we have the whistle, we can go," Earl said. "No reason to stay here all weekend."

"Do you think they're getting close?"

"Yes. When I asked Cayson for the laptops, he said they were close."

"How close?"

Earl shrugged. "We could be here all weekend."

"Am I safe here?"

"Unless the FBI finds out that Stella has been asking questions. They come here to talk to her, they're going to find us in the building." Earl extended his hand. "Don't leave without me."

Sienna nodded. "I won't."

And now she had to keep her word.

They walked back to the table where they had left the laptops. Sienna logged in. "You sure this is secure."

"Yep. No one will know where you log in from."

Sienna checked her work emails. "Interesting."

"What?"

"Mr. Gavard is not cancelling the conference. It will start on Tuesday instead of Monday so we can all have a day to mourn." Sienna looked at Earl. "Monday. Only Mr. Ford's favorite day of the week."

"Really?" Earl chuckled.

"Really. He liked every day he made money." Sienna sighed. "I still need to go."

"Is Mr. Gavard expecting you? You're not his assistant."

Sienna didn't answer as she scrolled through the avalanche of emails that had flooded in. "Here's one from Noreen. She's Mr. Gavard's personal assistant."

She read the email and then summarized it for Earl. "She wants me to send her Mr. Ford's speech. Mr. Gavard is going to handle both the opening and closing remarks in Mr. Ford's place."

"So she's not asking you to fly there in person?" Earl asked.

"They asked, but I won't go." Sienna felt relieved that her job at GOOP was over. "I'm resigning."

"You told them?"

"Not yet. As soon as I have time, I'll sit down and write a resignation letter."

CHAPTER TWELVE

By the time Cayson cracked the whistle USB, it was past lunchtime. The whistle was a disappointment. Cayson promised to work on it some more, suspecting there were hidden files.

Reluctantly, Sienna left the USB with Cayson and his team.

When Deshon picked up Earl and Sienna from the Binary Systems headquarters in Alpharetta, Georgia, for their drive to Savannah and Tybee Island, it was three o'clock on a cloudy Saturday. Fortunately, it was still summer, and the sun wouldn't set until later.

Sienna was forever grateful that Earl had agreed to accompany her to Tybee Island.

Deshon came bearing gifts of new clothes from a nearby store. Earl and Sienna had ordered and paid for them online, and sent Deshon to pick them up.

After a late lunch of leftover Chinese food and pizza from the night before, they left the Binary Systems office in Alpharetta and made their way south through downtown Atlanta in the pouring rain.

Deshon was quiet at times, but at other times he liked to tell stories as he drove the rental SUV. Sitting in the front passenger seat, Earl kept cutting off Deshon whenever the latter had a story to tell. Sienna was irritated by Earl's interruptions, and she wasn't sure what had come over him. To his credit, Deshon took it all in stride, throwing smiling glances in the rearview mirror at Sienna every now and then.

Perhaps the content of the whistle USB had bothered Earl. Ever since Cayson and Leland had decrypted the USB drive, Sienna had been wondering what was going on. The conversation was clipped.

"Let's listen to the conversation one more time," Sienna said. "I don't recall Mr. Ford having a cold in the last couple of months. His voice still sounded odd to me."

"Didn't you say he was on vacation for a couple of weeks?" Earl asked. "Maybe he was sick on his vacation."

"He would've told me."

"Now we'll never know." Earl turned the volume up and tapped his phone. The conversation filled the vehicle.

> Gavard: Two weeks, Finn. Just two weeks.
>
> Ford: It matters not to me what you do. All I ask is you leave Dana out of it.
>
> Gavard: She's already in it whether she likes it or not.
>
> Ford: I don't think you heard me. Leave her out of it.
>
> Gavard: I've paid her. It's done.
>
> Ford: Tell me how much and I'll reimburse you.
>
> Gavard: You can't afford it.

Earl paused the recording. "We're missing lots of pieces."

Sienna agreed. "The missing segments could change its meaning altogether."

"If Dana held back the rest of it, then she's

complicit in something."

"I get the impression that she had been at the wrong place at the wrong time." As she said that, Sienna wondered if she believed it anymore.

Outside her window, a soft rain began to fall. A MARTA train whizzed by going the other direction next to the highway. The city carried on all around them.

"Or she planted her phone in the suite to record whatever went on while she was away," Earl said. "Randomly."

"Either way, she's in WITSEC and we won't be able to ask her," Sienna said. "Let's hear the other segment."

Earl nodded. "I have some theories about this one."

> Ford: I'll go to your wife.
> Gavard: Too late. She already knows.
> Ford: She does?
> Gavard: Yep. And she wants me to
> clean up this mess or she's
> getting a divorce after
> Christmas.
> Ford: It's your fault you don't have a
> prenup.
> Gavard: I don't care. I have Dana.

> Ford: Only because I let you
> have her.
> Gavard: You moved on to that mail-
> room clerk.
> Ford: She has a name, okay?
> Genevieve.
> Gavard: Whatever. Thanks, little
> brother.

"Let me take a stab at this." Deshon tapped on the gas pedal as they left Buckhead and traffic picked up as Highway 400 merged into Interstate 85, which was also Interstate 75. "Those two brothers fell for the same woman, Dana, but the younger brother conceded to the older brother."

"That was my guess too." Earl fist-bumped Deshon.

"Let's see whether Helen has a different take on the analysis," Deshon said.

"Speaking of whom, Helen wants me to ask if you've thought of working full time for Hu Knows. Part-timers get part-time fun, you know?"

"Is she thinking of sending me to the Savannah office?" Deshon asked.

"To start with. Technically, there would only be three PIs in Savannah if you come onboard: you, Cade, and me. The rest are at large or in Europe."

"Let me ask you something," Deshon said.

"Sure." Earl put away his phone.

"Why does Hu Knows have two offices in Europe? Why not consolidate Brussels and Athens?"

"Good question. Helen is in Athens because her mother is in jail there. When she gets out, Helen has to stay in Europe because her husband is an ex-con and he can't yet get a visa to come here."

"Europe sounds nice."

"I used to envy Hugo when Helen sent him to run the Brussels office," Earl said. "There I was, stuck in an old office in Savannah. Now I don't want any of the European assignment. I mean, I want to go there on vacation, not to work."

"Makes sense. So have you gone?" Deshon asked.

"I was supposed to this week," Earl said quietly.

"Oh." Sienna gasped from the backseat. "I ruined your plans. I'm sorry."

"No, it's not your fault," Earl replied. "I can always take another vacation. You can't always have another life."

"You get to spend time with me—a woman on death row."

"You won't be if we take care of your enemies." Earl sounded determined.

"Only God can take care of my enemies." Sienna reminded him.

"Yes." Earl nodded. "And when this is over, we could make a trip to visit Europe, whoever wants to go."

Sienna raised her hand. "I want to see the world if I make it out of Tybee Island alive."

"I suspect that the Brussels and Athens offices might merge someday." Earl speculated.

"Then where would Hugo go?" Deshon asked.

"I don't know this for sure, but I am guessing that Helen would let Hugo run the one office, and she would just float among the branches. She prefers to work at home, and she doesn't really care for office work like administrative stuff."

Sienna's ears perked up as she listened to the guys talk. "I love admin stuff. Don't tell me you don't have an office manager for Hu Knows?'"

"You'd think that with such a growing company, we would." Earl chuckled. "However, Helen is a control freak, and no office manager or administrative assistant has lasted over six months."

"Sounds like a challenge," Sienna said.

Earl turned his head slightly. "You want the job? You could apply and see what Helen says."

"If GOOP goes down, I'll be out of work soon,"

Sienna said frankly. "I still have expenses, with Mom's care."

"I hear you," Earl replied. "Say, have you considered applying to the Savannah Senior Living Resort on Tybee Island?"

"I heard of it, but it might be too expensive for me."

"If you work at Hu Knows, you can probably afford it," Earl said. "Besides, they also give discounts to veterans."

"They do? My Uncle Tabbebo is a Navy veteran."

"That's cool," Deshon chimed in. "Where did he serve?"

"He was injured in the Korean War. He rarely talks about his experiences, so we never ask. Now he's taking care of Mom, his only sister." Sienna tapped Earl on his shoulder. "What about you? Did you serve?"

"Army Special Forces." It was all Earl said.

"Well, I was in the Girl Scouts," Sienna said. "Troop leader."

"That's noble," Deshon said.

"Right. Very noble," Earl echoed. "Have you ever gotten into trouble, Sienna?"

"Well, when I was four years old, I burned down my dad's barn," Sienna said.

Everyone laughed.

"Where was that?" Earl asked.

"North Georgia. Outside Dahlonega."

"So you're from there?"

"No. My family is from Savannah," Sienna explained. "When I was three years old, my parents divorced. Dad moved back to his family farm in North Georgia. Mom stayed in Savannah, where she met Mama Hu and her family. I was in preschool and then kindergarten, so Mom didn't want me to move around the country. She waited until I was in middle school and then she took off. I stayed with Mama Hu until I graduated from high school."

"Where did your mother go?" Earl asked.

"I found out later that she was in jail. She was serving time. She couldn't even go to my high school graduation. I hated her for it until I found out what happened." Sienna blinked. She did not want to talk about it any more. "How far are we from Macon?"

"An hour and half from Midtown," Deshon said. "If it makes you feel any better, I was adopted."

"Really?" Sienna asked. "Ever thought of finding your biological parents?"

"Nope." Deshon drove into traffic heading

toward downtown Atlanta. "How did you end up in Savannah, Earl?"

"Well, it was a career move. After my Army days, I needed a job," Earl said. "Helen was looking for a former Special Forces with a particular skillset."

"What kind of skillset?" Sienna asked.

"I do everything."

"That's all you'll say?"

"That's all I can say." Earl's voice sounded serious.

"Is that why the FBI allowed you to tag along with her?" Deshon asked. "I mean, don't they usually use their own undercover agents?"

"Two words: budget cuts," Earl said.

"Oh, and here I thought Helen pulled strings." Deshon chuckled.

"Strings?" Sienna said. "To me, their strings are not connecting. There are knots. And some parts are cut."

"And we don't know who is pulling the strings," Earl added.

"Right." Sienna looked outside the window. They had just driven past Georgia Tech to their right, and were heading toward the center of the city. Traffic wasn't as bad as weekdays, but they had a long way to drive yet. She leaned against her seat back and wondered if she could take a nap all the way to the Georgia coast.

"Based on everything we know about the case, who do you think is pulling the strings?" Earl asked. "Deshon, you start."

"On the outset, it seems that Gavard is in charge, from the way he talked down to his brother," Deshon said. "However, it's entirely possible that Ford is the wizard."

"Sienna?" Earl asked. "Thoughts?"

Sienna appreciated being included in the assessment even though she wasn't a private investigator. However, she had access to data pertaining to the case. "I don't know, to be honest. I do know that I don't trust Agent Kimball."

"Neither do I, even though Stella told me to trust Kimball," Earl said. "I don't know if I can, to be honest."

"You asked her out to dinner," Sienna countered. "So you must trust her to some degree, right?"

Deshon laughed. "He asks everyone out."

"He sort of asked me out too," Sienna said. "Although we already are pretending."

"At least we're not pretending to be married," Earl said.

"Speaking of which, if you do get married, will you still go undercover like this?" Sienna asked.

Earl shrugged.

"What would your wife say?"

"I won't know until I get there," Earl said.

"Do you think you'll ever get there?" Deshon asked.

"Sure," Earl said. "Someday, I want to settle down and have kids. God will show me who my true love is."

"Oh, a hopeless romantic former Special Forces hero." Deshon glanced at his colleague. "Are you blushing?"

"I'm not." Earl cleared his throat. "Hey Sienna, I wanted to ask you about sharing a suite at the conference instead of being in two separate rooms. I can't protect you from a room down the hallway."

"I don't know." Even though she trusted Helen —and therefore, she had to trust Earl—Sienna wasn't sure about taking their fake relationship that far.

"Maybe they have adjacent suites with a door in the middle," Deshon suggested.

"Good idea," Earl said. "I'll ask Cora. She knows we're coming."

"Thank you, Earl," Sienna said.

"Don't worry. Our job is to make sure you don't get killed."

Deshon chuckled. "You might get hurt, but we won't let you get dead."

"Yeah, our jobs are not easy," Earl explained. "We get paid to do this, so I hope you don't get the wrong idea, Sienna."

His voice sounded genuine.

"Don't worry about it." Sienna drew a deep breath. "When this is over, they'll put me in WITSEC and you'll never see me again."

"If we catch the criminals who are pulling the strings, you might be able to live free and not have to change your identity," Earl said.

"Speaking of WITSEC, is it possible to find out where Dana is?" Sienna asked.

"No. The US Marshals know, but we won't."

"Something is not adding up." Sienna closed her eyes. Tried to recall her visit to Dana the day before. "Why did the FBI take that moment to whisk her away to WITSEC?"

Suddenly she realized it. "It was me. I brought her would-be killers to her house."

"I would imagine they already knew where she lived."

"I don't know, Earl. It was her hideout."

"Her own safe house?" Earl chuckled.

"With a would-be assassin at the kitchen window and a gunman who walked toward Sienna in the living room and asked for the whistle."

"Good questions," Sienna said. "Hopefully, we'll get some answers once we get to Mr. Ford's beach house."

"Is there another way?" Deshon asked.

Sienna shook her head. "The safe is in the basement of the beach house. He gave me—and apparently only me—the combination."

"Why?" Earl asked. "Why you?"

"Because he trusted me," Sienna said.

"Still, we'll need some help if we get ambushed." He turned to Deshon. "You sure you can't come? Cade and I could use an extra hand."

"I wish I could." Deshon kept his eyes on the road.

"No, he can't come," Sienna said. "He has to feed Wyclef."

"Important job," Deshon said.

"You have no idea. You're my hero because you're taking care of my cat. If I could bring him with me..."

Earl cleared his throat. "No cats—or pets—allowed on this business trip."

A car horn startled Sienna. Someone had

improperly changed lanes. "Whew. That looked like a wreck almost happened."

Above the highway, planes crisscrossed the sky of Atlanta outside the Hartsfield-Jackson International Airport. One hour to Macon, and three hours closer to the island of reckoning.

Deshon would be leaving them in Macon and driving back to Sienna's house to feed her cat. In Macon, they'd hop in another car and drive to Savannah. They would get there before dinner and it would still be Saturday.

"When we get to Macon, I don't mind driving," Sienna offered. "I know the way to Savannah and Tybee Island."

Neither Earl nor Deshon said anything.

"Are you afraid I'd drive somewhere else?" Sienna asked.

"I want you in the backseat so you don't get picked up by the street cameras." Earl swiped his phone. "Cade will be waiting for us in Macon. He'll follow our rental car just in case."

"Are you expecting trouble on the road?" Sienna asked.

"Yes, since we don't know who your enemies really are."

Sienna nodded. She prayed for God to show her who the enemies were. Like Deshon said earlier, the most obvious people were Gavard and Mr. Ford. With Mr. Ford dead...

Why would Gavard come after her? Dana hadn't told Sienna enough to make the latter an enemy to the executives. Gavard was more a salesman, carrying GOOP to the multi-billion dollar company it now was. Ironically, he wasn't the majority partner.

With Arun and Rocco dead, dare Sienna put Dana on the lineup? Dana had been her friend for over three years. Even though Dana had problems, Sienna could not imagine that Dana could be an enemy, even though Sienna was disappointed that the whistle USB yielded nothing of substance. She had been half-expecting a list of names or transactions.

Sienna watched the trees and forest whizz by outside the vehicle as they headed south toward Macon. Traffic cleared. Ahead of them were a long road and open skies.

Deshon and Earl chit-chatted and listened to talk radio with more commercials than there was substantive conversation.

Sienna ignored the men as she continued to stare outside, praying for God to show her what to do next.

She began to regret going to the FBI about what

she had seen and heard. It had prompted a whole slew of investigations that had done nothing so far.

Who embezzled money from GOOP? What were the shell companies? Sienna wished she had taken a photograph of Dana's screen on her phone. Now she could not remember exactly what the company names were.

She closed her eyes to try to recall what she had seen. It had been three or four months back. She could recall nothing.

She felt trickles of tears coming down her cheek and quickly wiped them away.

"You all right?" Deshon's eyes met hers in the rearview mirror.

"I'm okay. Thank you."

Earl turned his head. "Sienna?"

"Thank you, guys, for caring," Sienna said. "I'll be fine when all this is over."

"Hopefully soon." Deshon pointed to a turn in the road coming up. "We're almost at the rental car place."

Earl texted on his phone. "Cade is already there."

"Good. Then you don't have to wait for him," Deshon said.

Interstate 75 split into Highway 16, and Deshon drove on the latter. Turning right on

Spring Street, the vehicle crossed the Ocmulgee River. Deshon zigzagged here and there on the rectangular streets of downtown Macon until they reached the car rental place.

As soon as they pulled into the parking lot, a swarm of vehicles surrounded them, blocking them in such that the SUV could not go forward or back or even sideways. Some of the vehicles were local police cars. Some had no markings. Armored personnel jumped out of the vehicles and pointed weapons at their SUV.

"What's happening?" Sienna asked.

"I don't know." Deshon parked the vehicle, and placed both hands on the steering wheel.

Behind the wall of armed law enforcement officers, someone emerged.

Someone familiar.

Oh no.

CHAPTER THIRTEEN

FBI Special Agent Mariana Kimball sent Deshon home, and ushered Earl and Sienna into an unmarked van. The driver was the same guy who had driven them from Dana's house to the first safe house.

This time, Kimball climbed in after Earl and Sienna. Clearly unhappy with her civilian runaways, Kimball chewed a giant wad of nicotine gum furiously.

The van was going somewhere southbound. Earl asked, but Kimball wasn't taking questions.

She was sitting across from them in the van. Earl and Sienna sat on one side on a bench seat, and held hands until Sienna stopped shaking. They had been shaking since they left the rental car place.

"You knew better than to pull this on me," Kimball said.

Earl didn't deny her statement. He was willing for all of the blame to be upon him as long as Sienna got a break from Kimball. Neither of them trusted the FBI agent, but with at least twenty LEOs surrounding them, there was nothing Earl could do but surrender Sienna to them.

Kimball shook her head at Sienna. "Looks like you want to go to jail, woman."

"I'm trying not to get murdered, like Agent Perez at the safe house," Sienna replied.

Kimball's eyes flickered. "That was unfortunate. Don't make my job any harder."

"Mr. Ford is dead." Sienna sniffled.

"I know. So are Rocco and Arun. Do you want to be next?"

Even in her boots, Kimball was no more than five feet two. Right now, she looked small sitting there, yapping at them. However, she carried a big stick. With bullets.

Earl felt he had to be careful with her. Kimball was an FBI veteran and she was no joke. Perhaps she had made some mistakes in the operation. That could happen. Stella might be right about giving Kimball the benefit of the doubt.

"I'm trying not to be next." Sienna's voice was breaking, and that tugged at Earl's heart.

"Then help me help you. Why didn't you two go to the safe house?"

"Because of what you said on the phone." Earl would step in front of Sienna if he could, but with such a force around them, he decided to remain as he was.

"What did I say?"

"You said that Dana was at Grady. She wasn't, was she?" Earl asked.

Kimball was quiet, and then she drew a deep breath. "I lied to you. I didn't want to spook Sienna."

"Put me in WITSEC," Sienna said. "Let this be over."

"No, ma'am. You have to give us what we want, and WITSEC will be your reward. Just as Dana gave us what we wanted."

Earl didn't reply. What could he tell Kimball about Sienna's detour?

When Sienna also didn't say anything, Kimball continued. "You're flying to Freeport now. Your clothes from the safe house are in my vehicle over there. You're going to attend the conference. You're going to grieve with the Gavards and the GOOP family. You're going to listen with both ears and watch with both eyes, and report back to me."

Sienna didn't say a word.

"Oh, and to make sure you don't run off again, my agents are going to be all over that resort," Kimball said.

"Can you guarantee there won't be another Killjoy?" Sienna asked.

"She can't guarantee anything even if her life depends on it," Earl said.

Kimball raised her eyebrows at Earl. "I can guarantee you we will do our best, in the memory of Agent Perez. When this is over, and we've recorded your testimony, you can go free or go into WITSEC. I would prefer that you go free so that I can retire in peace and not have to revisit this."

"Retire?" Earl asked. "You're not even that age. You mean you're quitting?"

"This is my last operation. Agent Perez was my friend. It was my fault the safe house was ambushed." Kimball's face looked angry. "I want to go after Killjoy as much as you want to protect Sienna."

Earl wasn't sure how Kimball could compare the two, but whatever. "How did you find us in Macon?"

"We're not as incompetent as you think we are." Kimball glared at Earl. "I'm so disappointed in you."

"And I in you."

"I'm not playing games, Earl."

"Neither am I. You lost control of the operation when you let Killjoy infiltrate your ranks."

Kimball sighed. "You'll never let me live this down, will you?"

Earl ignored her question.

"Is Arun really dead?" Sienna asked. "Tell me the truth."

"Yes. He's in the morgue."

Sienna gasped. "Dana?"

"I told you."

"I wasn't sure I heard it right. She's safe?"

"Yes, she is. But you'll never see her again. That's how it works." Kimball looked outside.

So did Earl. The van turned onto a road by a sign that said "Middle Georgia Regional Airport." Earl knew then that they were going to the Bahamas, after all.

"I'm resigning," Sienna said. "This is my last week on the job. Mr. Gavard wants me to turn everything over to his personal assistant, and then I'm done."

"One week is all we need." Kimball smirked.

Then she turned serious. "Dana shouldn't have given you the USB drive. She should have given it to me. Your error was in not turning that evidence over to us. However, going to Binary Systems turned out to be just what we need."

Earl glanced at Sienna. She didn't look at him.

"That's how we tracked you down," Kimball said. "Thank you for getting the whistle decrypted for us."

Earl figured it had to be Stella who had helped Kimball connect the dots. Even if she wasn't working with Kimball, Stella had been calling around to look into Dana Nesbitt's whereabouts. Word would get back to Kimball.

"Surely Dana had given you the same data," Earl said.

"What she gave us was incomplete. Enough to get a wiretap but not enough for an arrest warrant." Kimball pointed a finger at Sienna.

Sienna recoiled.

"Now, you are going to get us the rest of the information," Kimball said. "Let's just say you need to make up for withholding evidence from us."

"Please don't scare her," Earl said.

"Does she look scared to you?" Kimball snapped. "She's braver than you give her credit for."

The van rolled to a stop near the runway, where a private jet was parked. It looked like a Citation XLS. A mid-range jet, it could easily fly them to Freeport, which was only about four hundred and fifty nautical miles from Atlanta.

"Is that our ride?" Earl wondered how the rest of Kimball's team would get to the Bahamas.

"Your taxes at work." Kimball opened the van door.

"How many people does it seat?"

"Eight. The rest of my agents are already in the Bahamas. They took the same flight as Mr. Ford this morning."

As they filed out, Earl turned to Kimball. "Did someone kill Finnegan Ford?"

"The matter is still under investigation. I would like to add murder charges to Gavard or whoever."

Earl realized then that Kimball was on their side, and that she had simply made a mistake with the safe house fiasco.

"I'm sorry I didn't trust you," Earl said to her.

"I'm sorry too. No dinner for you. Forget it."

Earl grinned. Not that he was going to ask her any more. The only person he wanted to have dinner with now was Sienna.

"Speaking of food, are we getting meals

onboard?" Earl asked as Kimball led them to the private jet.

"Sandwiches," Kimball replied. "This charter flight is costing us a fortune. You can eat a second dinner at the resort, courtesy of GOOP."

"Our last meals?" Sienna asked.

Kimball shrugged. "Life is perilous."

Earl held Sienna's hand as they walked toward the stairs. "You never thought that being an administrative assistant could be dangerous, did you?"

Sienna didn't smile. "Yet it's all in a day's work for you?"

"I'm happy we're still alive."

"Good. Stay positive." Kimball waited for them to board the plane before she herself got in.

They closed the jet door as everyone buckled in, except for Kimball, who took off her ballistic vest before sitting down.

Earl wondered if she was trying to show that she trusted them—or she knew she'd be uncomfortable buckled in while wearing the vest.

"How long is the flight?" Earl asked.

"About five hours." Kimball's seat was on the other side of the aisle, across from another FBI agent that she did not introduce to Earl or Sienna.

Sienna didn't say a word for most of the flight, eating in silence and saying grace on her own.

Earl could not read her face to get an idea of what she was feeling. Was she still shocked by the two deaths that had happened almost back to back: Arun the night before and Mr. Ford this morning?

Perhaps she needed grief counseling, something that Earl was not equipped to provide. He had lost friends in battle back in his US Army days, but for the most part, his life as a private investigator was less dangerous. Often called to do surveillance, he was away from the action in the European theater, where most of Hu Knows activities were these days.

That last time he had been able to do anything stateside, it was to work with a former FBI agent, who had to go to California to track down some lost treasures. Unfortunately, Earl was so shot up he spent a lot of time in the hospital, followed by weeks of recuperating on the beach on Tybee Island.

He couldn't complain, but after that he had sensed a change of attitude in himself. More mellow now, he had shed his party days. Still, that part of him which made quick decisions was still there. He remembered how his friends had laughed at him for falling in love quickly, only to fall out of love just as fast.

Across from him, Sienna pulled the blanket

over herself in the cool of the cabin. She peered over the top of the blanket and looked outside the window.

Earl had his own window, but all he could see were the wing and a bit of the sky. He stretched his neck a bit to see the land below. Just then, the pilot announced that they had crossed the Georgia-Florida line.

Across the aisle, Kimball was on her laptop, typing away furiously. Maybe she was writing a report. The other agent was fast asleep.

Earl checked his phone. There was Wi-Fi onboard, but he suspected that everything was monitored. He wasn't about to check his email and let his download stream be intercepted by the FBI.

He tried to recline his seat further, but it was as far as it could go. As he adjusted the pillow behind his head, Sienna got up from her seat and walked to the back of the airplane, where there were snacks.

Earl followed her. An FBI agent was leaning against the counter, checking his phone and eating a chocolate chip cookie.

Sienna looked through the tray on the countertop.

Earl stood next to her, mouth watering over the potato chips, brownies, cookies, sandwiches, nuts, and fruits, even though they had just eaten an early dinner.

"What would you like?" Sienna asked.

"What sandwich is that?" Earl pointed.

"Looks like ham and cheese." Sienna turned the wrapped sandwich over to read the label. "Yep."

"I'll have two of those, and a bag of potato chips I shouldn't eat, plus an apple—because I like to eat healthy."

Sienna chuckled. "I guess I'll do the same because we might die tomorrow."

The agent nearby looked in their direction.

"If you add too many calories tonight, will you still be able to fit into your swimsuit tomorrow?" Earl asked.

"I don't intend to swim, so I won't find out."

"No swimming in the Bahamas?" Earl opened the bag of potato chips. "Say it isn't so."

"What are you going to do while I'm at the conference?" Sienna handed Earl a napkin.

"Thank you. I'll be at the pool, talking to the spouses."

"You're getting paid for chatting with people."

"It's hard work."

"Uh-huh." Sienna opened the refrigerator. "Something to drink?"

"Water, please."

Sienna looked at the agent. "You?"

"No, thanks." He smiled.

Sienna smiled back.

Earl wanted Sienna to smile at him like that too. So he smiled to see how she would react.

She stepped closer to Earl and placed a hand on his arm. Earl felt warm all over. He didn't know why.

She found a plastic tray and filled it with what she wanted to eat. She handed another tray to Earl. No sharing. The tray was barely big enough to hold Earl's snacks plus soda and water.

"Shall we go back to our seats?" Sienna asked after they piled up their trays.

Earl nodded, walking behind Sienna. He glanced over at Kimball's screen. She was playing Solitaire.

When he sat down across from Sienna, he offered to say a blessing. Sienna nodded, and to Earl's surprise, she reached across the edge of the table to hold Earl's hand.

Her smile was genuine and warm and meant something. Earl almost forgot to pray. His mind went blank and he was losing his train of thought.

"Father God, we come to You, thanking You for the sandwiches—and snacks that we probably shouldn't feed our bodies—that we need to survive, or not." Earl cleared his throat. "Uh..."

Sienna retracted her hand. She began to pray. "Thank You, Jesus, for all that You have provided. In Your Holy Name, I pray. Amen."

"Amen." Feeling embarrassed, Earl didn't look at Sienna.

He had no idea what had happened to him. He felt that he was back in high school or college, falling in love for the first time—

What?

He nearly choked on plain bottled water.

"You okay?" Sienna asked.

No, I'm not okay.

He wasn't sure when things began to change between him and Sienna. One moment, he was trying to keep her safe. The next moment, his heart didn't feel safe from her.

Now he felt the urgency of having to keep her alive so that they could explore their relationship more. Yet they were flying into the fiery furnace, so to speak. What awaited them in the Bahamas?

"Tell me about your family," Sienna said as she munched on what looked like sweet potato chips.

"My parents are retired from their careers in the Army, and they live in Charleston, where they run a bed-and-breakfast," Earl said.

"A second career, huh?"

"I don't know how long they'd do that. They don't need the business." He drank more water as he looked at Sienna. "My three brothers are all over the place, but once a year we go home to Charleston for Thanksgiving."

"Nice."

"I gather you go to Chattanooga to see your mom a lot?" Earl said.

"I was until the last few months when I was caught up in this web." Sienna paused. Folded the empty chip bag. "Thank you for getting someone to keep my mom and uncle safe."

She remembered.

"No problem." Earl dug in to his cold ham-and-cheese sandwich.

"How's that?" Sienna asked.

"Pretty good, actually."

"I think I had roast beef earlier." Sienna started on a small bowl of mixed fruits.

"Do you fly in jets like this with Mr. Ford?" Earl asked, and then remembered that Mr. Ford flew commercial. "Oh, he doesn't have his own jet."

"No," Sienna said. "Mr. Ford was a frugal man."

"Unfortunately," Agent Kimball said from

across the aisle. "All those billions, hoarded away in the bank, and now he's too dead to enjoy it."

"There's a lesson there, isn't there?" Earl asked.

"His two children will inherit the money via a trust fund," Sienna said.

"Good for them." Earl wondered what people did with all that income. "As for us, we have to work."

"Yeah."

"You might consider working with me," Earl said before he realized what he was asking. He recalled now that hours before, he had suggested Sienna apply to Hu Knows to work for Helen. Not with him specifically.

"You mentioned it. I'll pray about it."

"That's the best answer," Earl said.

CHAPTER FOURTEEN

E arl and Sienna arrived at Moss Grand Bahama after ten o'clock on a Saturday night that was bathed in a tropical downpour. While the rain lessened the humidity outdoors, the resort was cooler inside.

Kimball and her team blended into the surroundings, causing Earl and Sienna to check in on their own. At least they had their luggage with them, which Kimball's people had brought from the safe house back in Atlanta.

Sienna was thankful to God that the receptionist found them two connected suites. Normally reserved for larger families, the suites came with a drawback: they were five floors up and faced the parking lot instead of the grand Caribbean ocean. A fast getaway down the elevator or a mad dash down five flights of stairs wasn't going to happen.

Still, it made Sienna feel better that Earl was her neighbor, separated only by an interior door. That way, she didn't have to go out to the hallway to knock on his door to call for help—should the need arise.

They came up the elevator together, and then Earl told her to stand at the door while he checked the room. He used his phone like a scanner in front of him. After a few minutes, he returned to the front door.

"No bugs. You can go inside now," Earl said.

"Thank you, Mr. Paranoid." Sienna saw that the connecting door was ajar. "I assume you've scanned your own room for bugs too."

Earl nodded. "Can't be too careful."

By the time Sienna rolled her carryon to the closet, she was spent. However, she had to check in at work. Using the secure laptop that Kelvin at Binary Systems had set up for her, she logged in to find an avalanche of new emails from Gavard's personal assistant, Noreen.

She replied to the most urgent ones, especially about the conference starting on Tuesday instead of Monday to give the GOOP family an extra day of mourning before they got back to business. Gavard didn't want to skip a beat even though he had lost his half-brother tragically on Saturday morning.

It made him a suspect.

Or at the least, heartless.

As soon as Sienna sent the email, she received a terse note from Noreen asking Sienna to call her back. Sienna took a deep breath and tried to remember what her cover story was regarding her misplaced phone.

The resort phone would have to do for now.

"Hey, Noreen," Sienna said as soon as Noreen picked up.

"Where have you been, girl?" Noreen's high-pitched voice couldn't get any higher.

"I just arrived this evening."

"What happened?"

"I missed my flight on Saturday morning. Over-slept." It was the truth.

"You never oversleep. What happened?"

"I had a late night on Friday," Sienna said. "My boyfriend and I were up half the night, and then I couldn't get up."

"You had a first-class ticket."

"I know. I wish I had been there. Maybe Mr. Ford wouldn't have..." Sienna blinked

"It's terrible. It's sad, but such is life. If you like, I'll ask Mr. Gavard to give you a good referral."

Sienna shook her head. "I just want to get through this week."

"It's your last week at GOOP, but you'll still get paid. All is not lost."

"At this point, I don't care about my job. I just feel sorry for Mr. Ford's children."

"Oh, yes. Them too," Noreen said. "Listen, Mr. Gavard wants to meet with you Sunday afternoon. He has to make the opening remarks on Tuesday and the closing remarks on Thursday. That's on top of his own keynote address on Wednesday. He's all stressed out. The poor man. He's upset his brother died on him at this very bad time."

"Like Mr. Ford should have waited until after the conference before he had a heart attack?" Sienna wondered where Mr. Gavard dug up Noreen. She was just as heartless as him.

"Well, what's done is done," Noreen said. "Don't forget. Three o'clock Sunday afternoon. Meeting Room Seven. Can you make it? Don't oversleep."

"I don't nap in the afternoon."

"Good. Bring all your notes for Mr. Ford's speech. Mr. Gavard might just have to go with them since it's the last minute, you know."

"Right." Sienna said goodbye.

The good thing about Noreen—and hopefully

Gavard—being focused on themselves was that they didn't bother to ask Sienna detailed questions about what happened to her on Friday and Saturday. In fact, Noreen didn't ask about Dana or Arun.

Sienna shut down her laptop. She washed her face, brushed her teeth, showered, changed into her pajamas, and climbed into bed with her Bible.

The knock on the connecting door next to her bed came just when she was about to fall asleep with her hair wrapped up in a bath towel.

She texted Earl, asking if it was him.

EARL

Yes, it's me. Just making sure you lock your other door.

SIENNA

I think I did.

EARL

Go check.

SIENNA

I'm in bed. Why don't you go out to the hallway and check my door for me?

She was half jesting, but Earl did not reply. Next thing she knew, someone was knocking on her front door. She could see the knob jiggle. The door did not open.

Sienna got out of bed, padded to the front door, peeked through the keyhole, and opened it. Sure enough, it was Earl.

"You shouldn't open your door all the way," Earl said. He was wearing a black tee shirt and a pair of jeans.

"Since there's no chain latch, I wouldn't be strong enough to hold the door in place if someone were to push in." She stepped aside to let Earl in, and then locked the door behind him.

"Keep your phone charged up," Earl said. "That way, if we need to talk to each other or if you need to call for help, you have battery."

"However, if there's no signal, what good is a fully charged phone?"

"I just want you to be safe."

Sienna sighed. "Sorry I sound cranky. I'm tired, is all. Long day."

"Long day for me too."

Sienna realized she had been a little selfish. They were both tired. She followed Earl to the connecting door. "Earl?"

He stopped and turned toward her.

"Thank you." Sienna reached for his face with one hand, and planted a gentle kiss on his cheek.

Without a word, Earl held her hand. Sienna responded by placing her head on his shoulder.

The hotel towel fell off, and her damp hair brushed against her arm.

When Sienna stepped away, she saw that the water from her damp hair had seeped into his sleeve. She pointed. "Sorry."

"It'll dry." Earl shrugged. "What are you doing for church in the morning?"

"You heard Agent Kimball. Under no circumstances are we supposed to leave this resort until Thursday."

"Yeah. I checked with the concierge and there's no chapel on site. There are churches in Freeport, including Freeport Chapel by the Sea, which is a sister church to one in Nassau. My church has sent mission teams to help them with summer camps and vacation Bible school."

"All outside the resort," Sienna said. "I was thinking of live-streaming the church service from Midtown Chapel. If you like, we can watch it together at breakfast. There are two services."

"My church has two services too."

"Right. Riverside Chapel. I haven't been there before."

"Maybe when you visit Savannah, you can drop in."

"Sure. What time is your service?"

"Eleven in the morning," Earl said. "For tomorrow, I guess we could watch our own church live-streams, or we could get together?"

"I'll watch your church service with you. Where shall we meet?" Sienna asked.

"Here or in my room. Either way."

"Here, then," Sienna said. "I'll have coffee ready."

"Shall we order breakfast for ten o'clock?"

"Sounds good to me. There are no activities until Tuesday."

"Tuesday? I thought we hightailed here because the conference starts on Monday."

"It was, but Mr. Gavard is giving everyone an extra day to mourn."

"How nice," Earl said. "So how is GOOP planning to mourn?"

"There's nothing scheduled for Monday. It's an off-day. No memorial service or anything. Each of the hundred-plus attendees will mourn in his or her own way."

"Like at the pool and in the ocean?"

"Mr. Ford wasn't exactly well-liked at GOOP," Sienna said. "However, some think that Mr. Gavard is worse. He has security around him because he's afraid someone might hurt him."

"Speaking of security, I have a meeting

tomorrow after church with the chief of security here," Earl said.

"You know Mr. Jones?"

"How did you know his name?"

"Mr. Ford had me call him last week. He was worried about coming here, but then after he talked to someone at the security office, he decided he was just being paranoid."

"And then he died before he got here."

"I didn't think he should have worried," Sienna said. "Moss Grand Bahama is the resort of the rich and famous. I'd be surprised if Mr. Gavard and Celestia didn't pick this place themselves."

Earl agreed. "Two thousand dollars a night isn't for everyone."

Sienna wondered. "Did Helen Hu pay for your room?"

"It's a part of the cost of keeping you safe," Earl said. "Do you have your watch?"

"It's in my purse." She lifted her right wrist. "Kimball insisted on putting the bracelet on me and she said I can take it off on Friday morning on the flight home to Atlanta."

"What about the other things she gave you?"

"The pen and clipboard are in my tote bag. I'm all set for the meeting tomorrow afternoon." Sienna rubbed her forehead with her fingers. "I'm tired, so I need to get some sleep."

"Good night. Sorry to keep you up," Earl said.

"Nothing to be sorry about. I feel safer with you here," Sienna said.

"Good. I've prayed that God will keep us both safe."

"Thank you." Sienna closed the door behind Earl. She didn't lock it, just in case.

At the same time, she reminded herself that she could not rely on Earl Young, a mere human being, to safeguard her, especially since they still had no idea who the enemy was.

Who had killed Mr. Ford—if he hadn't died of natural causes? The coroner's report would take at least a week.

Who had killed Arun?

And Rocco?

Ultimately, only God could protect Sienna.

CHAPTER FIFTEEN

After online church, Sienna went to her meeting with Mr. Gavard. Earl followed as far as he could go until he saw the security detail outside the meeting room.

Dressed in a tee shirt, a pair of swimming trunks, and a pair of flip-flops, he carried a bottle of sunblock. He looked like a typical tourist. Still, there was no way he could get past Gavard's security.

He went downstairs, sat in the lobby, and called Corazon Garcia-Moss to see if the chief of security of Moss Resorts was available to meet him at the security office. Corazon and her husband, Donovan, lived a few short miles from here in a gated beach community.

As soon as the phone started to ring, Earl regretted calling his former colleague at Hu Knows, Inc. It was Sunday, a day of rest. He tried to hang up, but someone answered the phone.

Corazon told him to go downstairs to the basement level of Moss Grand Bahama and wait for her. She would be able to get there in ten minutes. Right on the minute, she arrived. At eight months pregnant, Corazon could barely get through the door when she arrived at her office.

Earl gave her a hug around her belly. The baby kicked him. "Ouch."

"He's been kicking a lot," Corazon said.

"Feisty like his mama?"

Corazon chuckled. "Or strong like his daddy."

"How's married life?" Earl asked.

"Feels like we're still on our honeymoon." Corazon's face glowed.

"How long does that last?"

"I don't know. We've been married four years."

"Has it been that long?" Earl drew a breath.

"I know, right?" Corazon pressed a button on her phone, and someone knocked on the door in less than a minute.

She introduced Earl to the Moss Grand Bahama security director, a Mr. Jones with a thick

British accent. She used a remote to turn on several wall-mounted screens.

"I see the FBI agents," Corazon said.

"Yes, ma'am. They're in their own operational center."

"You gave them the second floor?"

"A few empty suites. They set up their surveillance teams there," Jones said.

"Where are all the GOOP people?" Earl asked.

"Scattered across the resort and surrounding villas," Jones said. "Security is tight, but many of them have brought their own security detail, so we try to work with them."

"Can you see everyone?" Earl scanned the screens.

"Everywhere but in their rooms and suites."

"Tell me where Sienna Halstead is," Earl said.

Jones didn't until Corazon gave him the go-ahead. "Give Earl what he wants. He's here in the best interests of his country."

Well, Earl only wanted the best interest of Sienna.

Jones took over the computer.

"Sienna called you last week on behalf of her boss, Finnegan Ford," Earl told Jones to establish some familiarity.

"Yes." Jones seemed to remember now. "I'm sorry Mr. Ford passed away."

"We're trying to get to the bottom of the mess," Earl said. "Anything you can help us with will be appreciated."

Jones pointed to a screen. Sienna was knocking on a meeting room door. On the door was the number seven.

"Is this live?" Earl asked.

"Yes, sir."

A woman opened the door for Sienna. Tall with too-tight clothes. She winked at the security guards standing watch. Then the door closed.

"That's Miss Noreen. She has talked to me a few times," Jones said. "Personal assistant to Zachary Gavard."

"Where's Mr. Gavard?" Earl asked. "And his wife."

"For that, we have to rewind." Jones made a quick work of it. He pointed to a series of videos. "Mr. Gavard."

As Earl watched the screen, he realized that Moss Grand Bahama used facial recognition to track its resort guests. "Is that legal?"

"It's private property," Corazon explained. "Last year, a trust fund baby was abducted from one of the nearby islands, and the parents sued the hotel chain for their lax in security. Donovan doesn't want us to be sued. Every guest has to sign a paper giving us permission to protect them."

"I didn't sign any. I don't think Sienna did either."

"Well, I saw your signatures," Jones said.

"Really?" Earl wondered if Kimball pre-signed it for them? That would run afoul of every law in the books.

Earl watched Mr. Gavard walk down the hallway, take the elevator, and reach the same meeting room that Sienna would enter an hour later.

"Where's his wife, Celestia Gavard?" Earl asked.

"She's here under Celestia Oppenheimer," Jones said.

"That's her maiden name."

Jones panned out the outdoor camera. "She's been at the pool all morning. She ate her breakfast there."

"I better find my swimming trunks," Earl said.

"Where's Dana, exactly?" Zachary Gavard —now the de facto CEO of GOOP— asked Sienna the second she stepped into the meeting room three floors below her suite. "Since she was let go, she has disappeared."

Noreen was sitting in another office chair next to Gavard. She wore a tight-fitting buttoned-down shirt with a row of buttons that looked like they were about to pop. In fact, the top three were already out of their buttonholes.

Surrounding them on the cherry table were paper, coffee cups, and laptops.

Sienna sat down on the other side of the table so that she could face the two of them. She was not within arm's reach of either one.

"I don't know where Dana is, sir," Sienna said. Gavard did not like Mr. Ford's employees to call him by anything other than *sir*. On the other hand, Noreen could call her boss by his first name, and nobody would bat an eyelid.

"You went to see her." Noreen pointed a pen at Sienna.

How did she know?

"When did I go?" Sienna did not bring a laptop with her because her work laptop was still in Atlanta. She placed her clipboard on the table, put the pen on top of it. She hoped they had started recording because she wasn't about to redo anything for Agent Kimball.

"I was just asking if you did," Noreen said.

Ah, fishing.

"I haven't seen Dana." Not since Friday. "Should I be concerned?"

"No idea." Noreen returned to her notepad.

"Where's your GOOP laptop?" Gavard said.

"Left it in Atlanta by accident."

"Never leave home without it."

"I'm sorry, sir."

"And you missed your flight," Gavard added.

"I told Noreen. I overslept."

"You were flying here with your boyfriend, right?" Gavard asked.

Sienna nodded.

"Who was picking up whom to go to the airport?"

"We were going together."

"From his house or yours?"

"Uh..." Sienna was stunned at what Gavard just asked her, even though she could not answer his question. There was no way she could tell him that they were at Binary Systems trying to read the USB drive from Dana.

"You finally have a boyfriend, and he's already leading you down the stray path," Gavard said. "I thought you were a Christian who doesn't sleep with your boyfriend."

"We didn't. We talked half the night."

"Right." Gavard shook his head. He mumbled something that sounded like *hypocrite*.

Here was the thing with him. He was obnoxious, but at least he spoke his mind.

Sienna started writing on the paper on her clipboard, fully aware that her bracelet from the FBI and watch from Earl were also probably recording. She prayed that Agent Kimball would be able to get enough evidence out of these conversations. She also wondered if they would hold up in a court of law, since they were surreptitious.

"Sir, I'm sorry about your brother," Sienna said.

Gavard nodded. "He lived a full life. His legacy will continue. We will carry on for his sake."

"Yes, sir." Sienna felt that GOOP had moved on from Mr. Ford, or at least his business partner here had.

"Did you send Finnegan's speeches to Noreen?" Gavard asked.

"Yes, I did." Sienna scribbled nonsense on the paper.

"She emailed it to me and I've printed them out. Here." As Noreen handed the printouts to Gavard, she leaned toward him such that it would be impossible for him to not see her cleavage.

However, to his credit, Gavard didn't look up.

He was busy highlighting another printout. "Put it right there. We need to discuss this first."

Such was the contrast between Gavard and Mr. Ford. Whereas the former preferred everything on paper, the latter had gone digital a few years before.

Then again, Sienna wondered if that might have opened doors to data fabrication. What if Mr. Ford hadn't been the embezzler?

What if it had been Dana all along? After all, Dana had been the company accountant. She knew every transaction, and she could fabricate any transaction if she wanted to. With the help of Arun, they could make it look like Mr. Ford had been embezzling money from the company coffers. Since Mr. Ford had conveniently died of a heart attack, the truth died with him.

Well, Dana wouldn't do such a thing to the father of her child, would she?

Sienna couldn't imagine Dana breaking the law and thereby losing her certified accountant license. If she had broken the law, why did the FBI agree to a deal with her? Why was she in WITSEC now as a protected witness?

"Mr. Lee doesn't like his villa because it isn't oceanfront enough," Gavard said. "He's texted me five times, threatening to pull out of the deal. I want him to buy those two hotels on Fifth Avenue because he's paying the highest prices for them. So make him happy, Noreen."

Noreen shifted in her chair. She pouted. "I'm helping you with your speeches."

Gavard looked directly at Sienna. "Can you take care of it?"

"Me?" Sienna wondered.

"Yes, you. It's your last week here. Noreen is busy. I want you to take care of Mr. Lee."

What did he mean by "take care of Mr. Lee"? Sienna's eyes widened.

"Just get him an oceanfront villa." Noreen waved her Christmas-red nails at Sienna.

Gavard put a checkmark next to the name. "Mr. Zhao needs a translator and an interpreter. His translator—who also interprets for him—has food poisoning and is sick in her room."

"What language?" Sienna scribbled herself a note.

"Mandarin Chinese."

Gavard stared at Sienna. "Can you make it happen? He's representing a conglomerate that wants to buy more land in the Midwest, and I have three hundred thousand acres in Texas I want to sell. I don't want Finnegan's death to block this sale."

"Monday?" Sienna asked. "That's tomorrow."

"Yeah. Oh, before you do all that, get us more coffee, will you?" Gavard pointed here and there. "And clear the table, please. I have a meeting with our real estate lawyers in half an hour. You know I don't like a mess."

"I didn't know that, sir." Sienna got out of her chair.

"You do now." Gavard laughed.

Without a word, Sienna threw out the used napkins. Slowly, she picked up the coffee mugs and small plates with crumbs on them as she glanced over at the printout in front of Gavard. It had colorful highlights on it. She wondered if it was the list of all the attendees—investors—of the conference.

"Can you speed it up? We don't have all day." Noreen smirked.

"I'm trying not to spill," Sienna said.

"Finnegan said you're very careful." Gavard looked at Sienna, but not at her face.

Sienna felt self-conscious, but she was modestly dressed, so she knew nothing was showing.

"Mr. Ford was a good man," Sienna blurted.

Gavard laughed so loudly that Sienna nearly dropped the cups in her hand. "Finnegan? That monster?"

Noreen rolled her eyes.

"He used to bully me all the way through high school, did you know?" Gavard thumped the table with his palm. His wedding band hit the cherry wood hard, and Sienna drew back.

"I was always behind him in everything. Father thought the best of Finnegan. Fifty-five percent of GOOP, can you believe it?" Gavard's eyes darkened. "I'm sorry he had a heart attack, but he did it to himself. He was always first in class, and now he's the first to die. Celestia and I are going to outlive him by many years."

"Yes, sir." Sienna cleared the table. She turned to Noreen. "Where's the coffee?"

"Down the hallway. Tell them to send a cart," Noreen said. "And then you better get going. Mr. Lee has been unhappy since he arrived yesterday. Nothing I've done appeased him. Maybe you'll succeed. You have a way with people."

"I don't know what that means, Noreen."

"Oh, you do. People seem to trust you," Noreen said just as the real estate attorneys showed up with two of GOOP realtors.

"Gentleman, you're early," Gavard said. "Noreen, we'll have to work on the speeches after we're done here."

"Okay." Noreen ushered Sienna out of the meeting room. She winked at the two security guards again. They barely smiled at her. "I'll take you to the coffee nook."

"Thank you. I've never been to this resort before so I don't know where anything is." Sienna laughed.

She had left her clipboard and pen on the table. She prayed that Gavard wouldn't discover what they were.

"Tell me about Mr. Lee and Mr. Zhao. If I know more about them, I might be more helpful," Sienna said.

"Is that how you're so successful with people that Mr. Ford never went to meetings without you?"

Sienna ignored her remark. "Mr. Zhao doesn't speak English, you say?"

"He speaks a little bit. He's from Shanghai, but growing up, he learned Russian instead of English." Noreen leaned closer to Sienna. "He's not allowed in the USA for some reason. That's why this year's conference is in Freeport instead of Atlanta."

"That doesn't sound good."

"It was Mr. Ford's idea to invite him."

"Blame the dead who can't defend himself?" Sienna asked.

"Mr. Ford wasn't Mr. Perfect. He left a messy

trail, like someone dragging a leaky trash bag across the carpet."

Sienna wondered who Noreen was parroting. She wanted to walk away, but Noreen was talking.

"You're saying that Mr. Zhao is Mr. Ford's guest," Sienna said.

"Yes."

"How come I didn't know about it? As his administrative assistant, I would have known."

"Not if you weren't in the office on Friday and he was working from his Tybee home."

"Friday?" Sienna asked. "That late?"

"Uh-huh. So hurry along and find Mr. Zhao a translator and interpreter."

"Is there one at this late hour?"

"Beats me. It's your problem now," Noreen said.

They stopped at the coffee nook. It was out of coffee. The attendant promised to get them more and have it sent to Meeting Room 7.

"What about Mr. Lee? Where's he from?" Sienna asked.

"Originally, he was from Hong Kong, but he's Canadian now. He wants to be a bigger partner than Mr. Gavard would let him. His company tried to buy the Empire State Building, you know?"

"I had no idea all these foreign investors are

buying up land and buildings in the United States," Sienna said softly.

"They've been doing it for years—decades."

"And that doesn't bother anyone in Washington?"

"Nope. You know how our real estate laws work. Anyone can buy land in the USA. You don't have to be an American or an American company."

Sienna nodded. "If the American economy tanks, foreign investors can buy up huge chunks of the country."

"And we'd all sell. Money rules."

"Money doesn't rule for everyone." Sienna tried to recall if Mr. Ford ever opposed any of the transactions.

"It most certainly did for Mr. Ford."

"Are you sure?" Sienna could vouch for Mr. Ford, but right now, she wanted to hear what Noreen had to say.

"For instance, Mr. Ford wasn't happy when he found out that Sweet Prairie LLC sold to an international conglomerate."

"Sweet Prairie?" Sienna was surprised. She recalled Mr. Ford calling the CEO his friend. The company owned many properties all over the country. Farmlands, city blocks, golf courses, you name it. And yes, Mr. Gavard and Mr. Ford each sold five percent of GOOP to them, which effectively gave them the same number of votes as Celestia. However, they would greatly expand their business. "They're still based out of Arizona, aren't they?"

"Yeah, but as of Friday, while you were out of the office, they were bought out by Evergreen November LTD in Cyprus."

"Never heard of it," Sienna said.

"Well, Mr. Ford himself found out about the sale one day before he died. He flew back to Atlanta from Tybee, and marched right into Mr. Gavard's house. You should have seen his face —uh..."

Silence followed.

Awkward.

"Only when Celestia isn't there," Noreen whispered. "Okay?"

Sienna wondered how Noreen could justify that. However, it wasn't her place to judge. "That's between you and God."

Someone exited the elevator. He was pushing a trolley with coffee and pastries on it.

"I better run." Noreen followed the trolley. "Meeting Room Seven."

Sienna wondered whether to retrieve her clipboard and pen from the meeting room. She texted

Agent Kimball, who was supposed to be somewhere in the resort. Kimball texted back instantly.

Leave it.

Sienna nodded to her phone. She took the elevator down to the lobby to find a way to move Mr. Lee to a better oceanfront villa. And she prayed for a miraculous solution to Mr. Zhao's language problem.

CHAPTER SIXTEEN

About an hour later, Sienna walked out to the pool and found Earl where he had said he would be. Under the shade of a giant umbrella, he was stretched out in a tee shirt and swimming trunks on a patio chaise lounge, chatting up none other than Celestia Gavard on the poolside lounge next to his.

Sienna hadn't seen Celestia since the GOOP Christmas party last December. At fifty five years young, she looked spectacular. Trim and tanned and athletic. A runner, the wife of Mr. Gavard could put everyone at GOOP to shame on the track.

Celestia made Sienna feel like she needed more exercise.

"Hello, Sienna," Celestia said. "You look pasty like you need some sun. I'll tell Zach not to work you too hard, especially now."

"I'm on my way back to the meeting room," Sienna replied. "Feels like I need to take a nap though."

"It's the heat." Celestia fanned herself. "I'm sorry about Finnegan. Such a dear man, gone too soon."

Sienna nodded.

"I was talking to your boyfriend here about how Zach and I met, and he was telling me how y'all met."

Sienna turned to Earl. "And what did you tell her?"

"Your Uncle Tabbebo set us up on a blind date, and we've been kissing ever since." Earl puckered his lips.

"Earl!" Sienna rolled her eyes. "Watch me not give him what he wants."

"I like you, Sienna." Celestia clapped her hands. "Come work for me. I need a good assistant. Finnegan told me you do great work. He gave you a raise every year."

Still standing in the sun, Sienna felt hot in her blouse and pants. She could jump in the pool if she had brought her swimsuit, but she had made a deliberate decision to leave it behind. She could always buy a new one in the resort boutique.

"I could use someone like you," Celestia said. "A no-nonsense type of worker bee."

"No nonsense because I refused to kiss my needy boyfriend here?" Sienna asked.

"Needy?" Earl's eyes widened. "I'm not needy. I'm quite independent."

Celestia laughed again. She looked at Sienna intently. "I'm serious. Zach doesn't need two assistants. I've read your yearly evaluations. You're loyal and everyone at GOOP respects you."

"Thank you for the compliments." Sienna smiled. "Let me pray about it first."

Sometimes faith could be a protective mechanism.

"You do that," Celestia said. "Pray and let me know."

Sienna respected Celestia more now because she did not mock Sienna's faith.

"On Monday night, I'm having a private dinner and dance at seven o'clock," Celestia said. "Would you two like to attend as my guests?"

Wow. Sienna had never been invited to any of Celestia's private dinners. She wasn't someone who invited non-peers to any of her events.

"Will your husband be there?" Earl asked.

"Maybe, maybe not," Celestia said. She looked unbothered. "If he feels like coming, he will. If not, he won't."

"It's nice that both of you have it worked out," Earl added.

Sienna didn't say a word. Although Celestia was a partner at GOOP, she did not hold a position at the office. Gavard attended most business events without her. In fact, according to Dana, Gavard often went on golfing trips without his wife. Somehow, they were still married after all those years of taking separate vacations.

"We both keep busy," Celestia said. "We won't miss each other."

Sienna wondered if she would miss her significant other if they were apart a lot. Well, first, she had yet to have a significant other.

Except this fake boyfriend right here.

Earl was grinning at her for some reason. "Are you going to change and join us?"

"Too hot for me." Sienna glanced at her watch. It was still afternoon, but she needed to go indoors where there was air-conditioning. "I'd better get back to the meeting room to see if they need me for anything else."

"Break's over, huh?" Earl asked.

Sienna nodded.

"I can't believe Zach made you work on a Sunday," Celestia said. "I'll need to talk to him."

"I'm not defending him or anything, but Mr. Gavard is making the two speeches that Mr. Ford was supposed to make, plus his own keynote address," Sienna said.

"That's just like him, that control freak." Celestia frowned. "He could've asked me, and I would've gladly spoken on behalf of Finnegan. We go back many years, he and I."

"You and Mr. Ford?" Earl asked.

Celestia nodded. "In fact, I knew Finnegan long before I met Zach. Finnegan and I went to the same college together. After college, I went to work for a PR firm, and Finnegan went to business school. When Finnegan turned thirty, he invited me to his birthday party, where I met Zach, and we hit it off. I can't believe they're half brothers. They aren't anything like each other at all."

Sienna knew bits and pieces about that, but she hadn't been paying much attention to anything related to Gavard. Standing there, listening to Celestia, she wondered how the GOOP partner ended up owning ten percent of the company shares.

Actually, it would be more now that Mr. Ford was dead. As far as Sienna knew, his fifty-five percent would be redistributed in equal percentages among the rest of the partners.

"How about a kiss for the road?" Earl suddenly asked, throwing Sienna off-guard.

When she regained her composure, she figured that Earl was trying to keep up their appearance to convince Celestia that he and Sienna were a genuine couple. Otherwise, word could get back to Gavard that some sort of scam was happening.

Then again, as far as Sienna knew, Earl had a cover. He had taken on the persona of one Earl Patterson, whose grandfather had passed away, leaving him enough fortune to be jobless and to travel the world. That way, there was little trail to go on if anyone tried to dig into his past.

"One for the road?" Sienna laughed. "All I'm doing is walking down that path and back to the hotel building. Not far. You'll see me tonight, Earl."

Earl lifted his sunglasses.

Sienna could not read his eyes. No Morse codes there.

He stared at her.

"Ah, whatever." Sienna stepped over to him. He smelled like sunblock. She lowered her face toward his, her hand on his shoulder. He reached out to hold her arm.

Under the umbrella in the hot sun, his lips were

warm and moist. They tasted like lemonade. His full lips fitted perfectly over hers, and they savored each other for longer than Sienna expected.

Earl moaned softly. His fingers were in her hair.

Slowly, she pulled away. "I have to get back to work."

"When do you finish?" Earl asked.

"I don't think it'll take long. There's nothing much I can do. Noreen's got it."

Hearing Noreen's name, Celestia made a face. "She's always got it. Wish Zach would fire her and hire you, Sienna. You're trustworthy."

"Noreen is not?" Earl asked.

"She's a gold digger. Doesn't care whose husband she beds as long as she gets to the top." Celestia's voice turned bitter and baritone. She seemed to catch herself as her broad smile returned. "Don't forget my dinner tomorrow night. White tie."

White tie? Sienna hadn't planned on wearing her gown twice this week. It had been folded up inside her carryon since the safe house. She thought she had time to get it to the resort cleaners for some quick steaming. Earl had rented a tuxedo—which he had packed away in his suitcase too.

As she walked away, she heard Celestia ask Earl what he did for a living.

"I'm in between jobs, and I'm tired of traveling the world," Earl said. "I'm thinking I would make a great bodyguard. You know, for something to do."

"That so?" Celestia's voice was back to sweet and sweeter. "I could use a bodyguard. Let me feel your muscles."

Gag.

Sienna tried not to react as she turned the corner on the path. She slowed down a little to hear what Earl had to say.

"Sorry, ma'am. That's a privilege only Sienna has." The wind carried his voice to Sienna.

Sienna reached a set of double doors.

A long arm reached around her and held the handle. "Allow me, ma'am."

Earl.

Sienna turned. "Aren't you supposed to be doing nothing by the pool?"

"Well, it's hot out there." Earl opened the door to let Sienna in. He walked in beside her.

"Is this 'take your boyfriend to work' day?"

Earl touched her jawline with the pad of his thumb. "May I have more?"

Sienna smiled and nodded.

He tilted his head and lowered his lips toward hers. He still tasted like lemonade.

The kiss was long, and time stood still all

around them. Work didn't matter. Danger didn't matter. Nothing mattered.

Sienna wrapped her arms around Earl's waist, and gently stroked his back. She could feel his muscles relax as he deepened his kiss.

"Oh, to be young and in love," someone remarked nearby. "Must be on your honeymoon."

When they came up for air, Earl whispered in her ear. "I meant that."

For a moment, they had not been pretending. Was this how it felt to be in love? Sienna wasn't sure. All of her past relationships had been short-lived, any passion brief and fleeting.

This time, it felt different.

There was something going on between her and Earl.

Someone tapped her on her shoulder. Sharp nails.

Sienna broke away from Earl to find Noreen shaking her head at them.

In her hands were Sienna's clipboard and pen. "You left these in the meeting room."

"Thank you," Sienna said. "I'm on my way back to the meeting."

"No need. The meeting is over," Noreen said.

"Oh."

"The lawyers left. I went over the speeches

with Mr. Gavard. All done now," Noreen said. "Did you get Mr. Lee and Mr. Zhou taken care of?"

Sienna nodded. "Mr. Lee is happy with the upgrade. Oceanfront suite with a butler and personal chef."

Noreen's eyes widened. "You're good. I would never have thought of adding a butler and a chef."

"Well, I've done that before to appease Mr. Ford's clients. Always give them something more."

"That's why you get bonuses every year."

Sienna shrugged. "Just doing my job."

"And Mr. Zhou?"

"That took a bit of work," Sienna said. "The physician on call here visited the translator and determined that she's better off at the hospital. At first the translator refused to go, but I arranged with the Moss Grand Bahama to get her secure video conferencing so that she could continue to translate and interpret for Mr. Zhou."

"So it worked out? Mr. Gavard will be happy to hear that."

"Turned out that the translator is Mr. Zhou's granddaughter. That would explain why he was worried," Sienna said. "However, the good physician worked at the hospital, so he got her a private room, and now Mr. Zhou has moved his office in there. He feels useful to be taking care of his own granddaughter."

"What does that mean?" Noreen asked.

"It means if Mr. Gavard wants to talk to Zhou, he'll need to drive over to the hospital."

"Okay."

"Either that or no deals with Mr. Zhou all week," Sienna added.

"I have to give you credit for that." Noreen sighed. "I was having a hard time with Mr. Zhou, and it wasn't just language barriers. You do understand people more than I do, Sienna."

"Just doing my job."

"Don't do too much, hear? Pretty soon you'd be taking my position." Noreen laughed.

"I don't want your job," Sienna said. "Don't feel threatened in any way."

"Good to know." Noreen strutted off.

CHAPTER SEVENTEEN

Earl combed his nearly-dried hair one more time, splashed on some eau de toilette, and whistled as he ambled toward the door separating his suite from Sienna's. What a fitting end to a long Sunday.

He still couldn't believe that she had agreed to have dinner with him tonight in the resort's only five-star restaurant on the other side of the outdoor pool. The restaurant was booked solid, but Celestia intervened and got them a balcony table for two at eight o'clock. Earl could not believe how nice she was.

Even though the door between his room and Sienna's was unlocked, Earl still knocked, as a courtesy to Sienna and a respect for her privacy.

No one answered.

He knocked again, placing his ear at the door. He could hear muffled sobs. Without hesitation, he flung the door open, and found Sienna sitting on the couch, and in tears.

She was trying to pull the bracelet off her wrist. "You can't do this to me! I'm not your prisoner!"

Earl could see that her wrist was red. The other wrist was empty. She had taken off the watch that he had given her, but the bracelet was still on her right wrist.

"What's going on?" Earl sat down next to Sienna.

Sienna lifted her wrist in the air. "I can't take the bracelet off. Agent Kimball locked it."

"It's waterproof, and you only need to wear it until Thursday night." Kimball's voice came out of a burner phone on the coffee table in front of them.

"I wasn't told. I didn't give you permission."

"It's for your good," Kimball added.

Earl snorted. "For her good? Or for your own purpose?"

"We all want to get to the bottom of the GOOP embezzlement. Two people have died, and there could be more," Kimball said. "She can help us save lives, or she can let more people die."

Earl was stunned at Kimball's statement. "I

can't believe you said that. Sienna is not responsible for your mistakes or other people's evil deeds."

He held Sienna's hand in his so that she didn't injure her own wrist any further.

"At least let her have a break," Earl said. "How about the night off? We're going to dinner."

"No." Kimball's voice was harsh. "She might run away."

"To where? We're on an island." Earl looked over at Sienna.

Her face was red, a sharp contrast to the light green floral dress she wore. Earl hated to see her in distress.

"I can't go out tonight," Sienna said. "Look at my wrist."

Earl sighed. "You ruined our dinner, Agent Kimball."

"You're not on vacation." Kimball hung up.

Earl drew Sienna to his chest. He knew that whatever they said could be heard by Kimball via the bracelet.

"What do you say to ordering in?" Earl asked. "We can ask them to set up a table for us, with candles and all."

Sienna nodded.

"We can watch a movie." Earl wasn't sure what she'd like to watch, but they could browse. That way, he could get to know more about her entertainment taste.

Sienna pulled away. She entered the bathroom and closed her doors.

Earl heard the faucet running and water splashing. She was probably washing her face.

He prayed that the operation would be over soon so that he could date Sienna properly without a sword of Damocles over their heads.

Date?

Did he hear himself say the word?

Sienna was still in the bathroom. Earl dashed back to his suite next door to get some antibiotic cream for her wrist. He returned as Sienna was coming out of the bathroom. Her face was freshly scrubbed. Her eyes were still red. The bracelet had rubbed her wrist raw.

In his hand were the cream and a menu. "I brought you some cream for your wrist."

"You're so kind," Sienna said.

"Sit down and I'll apply it." Earl followed Sienna back to the couch. Gently, he held her wrist with one hand and smeared a thin layer of cream on her skin.

"It's going to be all right," Earl said. "God is with us every step of the way."

Sienna nodded.

"If I could wear these for you, I would," Earl added.

Sienna blinked. "This must be how it feels to wear handcuffs."

Earl shrugged.

Sienna looked at him.

"What?" He asked.

"Nothing."

When he finished applying cream to Sienna's wrist, he picked up the menu he had brought from his suite.

"I have a menu too." She pointed to the refrigerator across the suite.

"How about we share this one?"

"Okay." She leaned closer to him.

He could smell lavender. Maybe a very light perfume. It went with her floral dress.

"What would you like to eat this evening?" he asked.

"Fish of some sort." Sienna pointed to the seafood column. "You?"

"Steak and shrimp. I'm famished."

They looked at the menu together. Earl put his arm over her shoulders, and kissed the top of her head. More lavender. "Did you use lavender shampoo?"

Sienna nodded. "Grilled cod. Maybe I'll get

that."

"And let's not forget desserts. Look at all that." Earl pointed to a whole page of decadent desserts.

After Earl had placed their order, they moved on to selecting a movie to stream on the big television on the wall.

"The other day, you told me that your date nights were usually movie nights at home," Earl said.

"You remembered." Sienna pulled away from Earl. "You know, 'the other day' was only two days ago."

"Is that right?" Earl shook his head. "So much has happened since then, but we're not talking about those things tonight. Right now we're taking a break from all that, okay?"

"Sounds good to me."

Earl clicked through the channels. There were action-adventure movies, period drama, crime fiction, romantic comedy, and so forth. The choices ran the gamut from one genre to another.

"What shall we watch?" Sienna asked.

"How about something light?"

"Something old or classic. A period drama, perhaps, that can transport us out of our present-day strife," Sienna said.

Earl handed her the remote. "Pick one. I don't

care."

All he wanted was to be with her, regardless of the movie they watched.

"How about historical fiction? Do you like Jane Austen?" Sienna asked.

"I've heard of her, but have never read her books nor watched her movie adaptations."

"Let's try this." Sienna highlighted it on screen. "*Pride and Prejudice*. This is one of the shorter remakes."

"Why not? Let's see the trailer." Earl waited as Sienna clicked and the video loaded. As soon as he saw the trailer, he knew it was romance. He didn't want to object to it because he was a romantic sort of guy too.

Except this evening he had forgotten to bring her flowers.

At least he was keeping her company, helping her cope with Agent Kimball's demands.

"Let's go with this movie," Earl said. "If I don't understand parts of it, you can fill in the blanks."

The doorbell rang. Earl told Sienna to stay on the couch as he went to check. He looked through the peephole, and saw a server wearing white. He opened the door.

Two people came in, placed a table cloth on a table already in the suite. They lit candles, and served Earl and Sienna until Earl sent them away so they could eat in private.

"Too bad we couldn't go eat in the restaurant," Sienna said. "It's amazing that Celestia could get us a table when we couldn't."

"Don't worry about it. You can be sure that they'll seat someone else there."

It was a lovely dinner, but truth be told, Earl would rather sit back on the couch with Sienna. He didn't care what movie they watched as long as he could put his arm around her shoulders.

"Let's eat our dessert while we watch the movie," Sienna suggested.

"Good idea." Earl followed Sienna back to the couch.

Sienna had ordered chocolate mousse cake. "Would you like a taste?"

Earl shook his head. "I don't share dessert forks."

Sienna chuckled. "Use your fork and get a piece at the edge."

Earl did so. "That is so...sweet. Try mine? Ground chicken inside."

"How can that qualify as dessert?" Sienna pointed to the pastry on Earl's plate. "It looks like an entire lunch."

"It can be." Earl yawned. What on earth? He

was feeling drowsy.

"Is the movie boring?" Sienna asked.

"No. I'm just... I don't know what overcame me. I feel very sleepy all of a sudden."

"Ate too much?" Sienna finished her cake and put the plate down on the coffee table. She leaned back against the couch, hands on her tummy.

The movie droned on while Earl could barely keep his eyes open. He glanced over at Sienna and she was fast asleep.

"Sienna?" He tried to wake her. She did not wake up.

He took her pulse. It was within an acceptable range.

Before he could try to wake her up, Earl felt dizzy. He blinked a few times as the room spun around him. The door opened, and shadows entered the room.

Then the whole world faded to black.

When Earl came to, he was alone in Sienna's room. Outside the windows, the sky was dark. He checked his cell phone clock. It was past two in the morning.

What happened?

He tried to get up from the couch, but his head was dizzy. It was as if he had ingested some potent sleeping pills.

The coffee table had been pushed aside, revealing an upside-down dessert plate on the carpet.

Earl got up, felt groggy, and sat back down again. "What on earth happened?"

He drew a deep breath and tried to get up again.

"Sienna?" Holding on to furniture, Earl called for Sienna as he walked from room to room, then to his own suite, and back again. "Sienna?"

She was nowhere to be found.

Using his burner phone, Earl called Kimball, but she did not pick up. He called Mr. Jones at the security office. Corazon had given him his phone number that afternoon.

"Gone. I woke up and she was gone," Earl told Jones.

"We will search for her straight away."

"Thank you, Mr. Jones. I think you might want to send a security team up here to gather evidence. Someone might have put sleeping pills in our food. We both passed out around the same time."

"Will do, sir."

"Are you going to be there all night?"

"I was leaving, but now I will stay," Jones said.

"Give me a few minutes and I'll be at your office." Earl didn't want to tell Jones on the phone that he saw shadows in the room before he passed out. He wanted to see who had entered the room.

"Anything else, sir?"

"Working on the assumption that she has been abducted, you need to call the local police for help," Earl said. "Do they know that FBI agents are in town?"

"Yes, sir."

"Where's Agent Kimball?" Earl asked, walking down the hallway outside the suites, his phone glued to his ear.

Jones took a while to scour the videos for him. "Their team left the resort two hours ago."

"No kidding. The entire team?" That was odd. And it would explain why the FBI hadn't come running to their suites.

"Nine people in two vans. Valet cameras," Jones said. "Could they have taken Sienna?"

"I don't know." It wouldn't make any sense. The FBI wanted to...

Oh.

The tracker that Kimball had put inside Sienna's bracelet would tell them where she was. Had Kimball and her team left to follow her?

JAN THOMPSON

Unfortunately, Sienna wasn't wearing the watch that Earl had given her. Now he couldn't track her down.

Earl knocked on the security office door. Someone opened it. "I'm here to see Mr. Jones. He's expecting me."

"This way, Mr. Peterson."

Earl didn't correct him.

"The police officers are on their way." Jones waved him over. "We're looking at all the security cameras for the coming and going of anything from eight last night until now."

"Thank you." Earl sat down. He still felt a little dizzy.

"Would you like some water?" Jones asked.

"Yes, please."

Jones waved to someone to bring Earl a glass of water. Earl thanked him and drank it up.

Earl called Kimball again.

No response.

He called Helen Hu. Told her everything.

"Let me process this," Helen said from her home in Greece. "What kind of bracelet?"

Earl didn't know. "I should've taken photos."

"RFID? GPS? What?"

"No earthly idea."

"So we have to find another way to get to those

212

trackers—assuming they're still on her."

As Earl listened to Helen, he realized he knew how to get to Sienna.

"Helen, could you work on the Kimball angle? Maybe talk to the Special Agent in Charge about her tactics? They're brutal," Earl said.

"I'll do that. I'm calling Espy. You remember her?"

"Good idea." Esperanza Diaz-Mendenhall owned a security firm that sometimes gave Hu Knows a hand whenever they needed paramilitary help. "Ask her to be on standby in case we need a rescue team."

"It will be costly, but Mendenhall Security is worth multiple times their weight in gold."

"First we have to find her." Earl thanked Helen. He held his head, praying the dizziness would go away. "Father God, help me find Sienna. Help me track her whereabouts."

Track...

Who was the best tracker Earl knew? There was only one. If anyone could hack into the FBI, pin down the signals coming from Sienna's bracelet and watch, and locate her point of origin, it would be her.

Earl speed-dialed hacker Leland Yang-Joule, and prayed she would be available at this hour.

CHAPTER EIGHTEEN

Sienna woke up, feeling the motion of the floor beneath her, and knew she wasn't on land anymore. She felt the same way she had a year before when GOOP took all the employees and their families on an Alaskan cruise.

A window showed her an unfamiliar ceiling of the outside hallway.

Where am I?

She tried to remember what happened, but all she could recall was sitting on the couch with Earl, trying to watch *Pride and Prejudice*, but never getting to the first scene.

Was it something she had eaten in the dinner?

She tried to get up but realized that her hands were tied behind her back and that she was not alone in the room. She tilted her neck to look up. She couldn't see anyone, although she heard soft sobs. Using her free legs, she pushed against the wall and the floor to try to get herself to sit up.

With great effort, she succeeded in sitting up only to find that her cellmate wasn't a stranger. "Genevieve, fancy meeting you here."

Genevieve wiped her eyes with her sleeves. Her hands were tied in front of her, unlike Sienna's. "Give them what they want and they'll let us go home."

"You know as well as I do that they won't let us go."

"I refuse to believe it."

"Believe whatever you want," Sienna said.

"You know the combination to Finnegan's safe." Genevieve's voice rose. "Give it to them, Sienna."

"I don't know what you're talking about."

"Yes, you do. Finnegan told me."

"Told you what?" Sienna looked around the box of a room, trying to figure a way out.

"That he gave you not only the combination of the safe, but the password to the laptop inside."

"Why would Mr. Ford tell you all that?"

"You're his insurance." Genevieve's voice steeled. "In his memory, don't let us both die."

Insurance?

JAN THOMPSON

When Mr. Ford asked her to his office several weeks before, he showed her a photo of the location of the safe in the basement of his beach house on Tybee Island. He told her that there was something he wanted her to do should anything happen to him.

He gave her the passcode to get into his house, the combination to the safe, and the password to access the laptop inside.

If anything should happen to Mr. Ford, Sienna would take the laptop to the authorities—notably the FBI.

Sienna had thought she was the only person Mr. Ford had told. Now she found out that he had told his girlfriend—the same woman now trying to do what the captors told her. If everyone who knew were to point their fingers at Sienna, she could be dead very soon.

"You're going to get us both killed," Sienna mumbled.

The door opened, and Joy "Killjoy" Burditt walked in, one handgun on each side of her belt, plus a sheathed knife attached to one thigh.

She said nothing to anyone. Her assistants went to Sienna.

"Talk to them, Sienna. Save us both!"

Killjoy's men helped Sienna to get on her bare

216

feet. She struggled to walk on the cold floor. They strong-armed her and led her outside.

Beyond the railings was the ocean, deep and wide. The sky above them was filled with clouds.

From the looks of the wooden deck floors, the railings on the side, the helipad on the other end of the vessel, Sienna guessed that this was a superyacht. If they could afford a superyacht, why would they bother wanting to break into Mr. Ford's safe?

Killjoy ushered Sienna down one flight of stairs and into a lounge surrounded by glass and windows.

There, sitting on a bright red settee, was none other than Celestia Gavard.

Sienna's jaw dropped. She glanced over at Killjoy, who remained with her. The henchwoman didn't talk much.

"Welcome to the Blue Sea Diamond, Sienna." Celestia smiled. "Nice to see you again."

"What's going on?" Sienna asked.

"Do you know how much this yacht cost me?"

Sienna ignored her.

"A hundred and five million dollars. That's how much."

At this point, Sienna was happy to let Celestia ask and answer her own questions.

Celestia nodded to someone nearby. He went

over to what looked like a rectangular side table with a black tablecloth on top, covering it all the way to the floor and then some. He pulled off the black tablecloth, revealing a safe.

It was about four feet high, and looked like the safe in Mr. Ford's beach house.

"Open the safe." Celestia pointed.

"Whose safe is this?" Sienna asked. At the back of her mind, she prayed that Earl would find a way to track her down and get her out of here.

"You know as well as I do that this is Finnegan's safe."

"Who brought it here?"

Celestia pointed to Killjoy, who nodded slightly.

"Now it's your turn," Celestia said. "The only person in the world Finnegan gave the code to is you."

Which made her valuable enough not to be murdered prematurely?

Perhaps she could use this to her advantage. If she could stall as long as possible, it could give time for Earl to find her. Maybe? Unfortunately, she wasn't wearing the watch he had given her. She knew she hadn't because she remembered leaving it inside her purse back at the hotel room.

"Why didn't Mr. Ford tell you the code to get in?" Sienna asked.

"He was going to. We were going to meet at Moss Grand Bahama and exchange information." Celestia shook her head. "He didn't make it out of Florida."

"So the secret dies with him."

"Unless he left the information with you."

"Find another way to crack the safe. I can't help you. I'm only an administrative assistant, not a safe cracker." Sienna knew there was danger to being a difficult hostage.

"Sit her down," Celestia ordered Killjoy, who pushed Sienna onto a couch.

Sienna tried to straighten up on her own. It was hard with both hands tied behind her back.

"Comfortable?" Celestia asked.

What was wrong with that woman? It was obvious that Sienna was not comfortable at all.

Sienna prayed for wit and tact and whatever other verbal weapon she could implement. At this point, she had to stay in the good graces of her captor.

"I can't believe I'm seeing you here," Sienna said. "I mean, you're worth billions of dollars. You don't need to do this."

"I've used it up." Celestia said as a matter-of-factly.

"Sorry?"

"I made some incredibly stupid investments and lost quite a bit of money, but primarily someone has been stealing money from my personal funds, and it's my own husband. Can you believe it?"

"Mr. Gavard?"

"He thinks I don't notice a billion here and a billion there."

"How?" Sienna found it hard to believe.

"Our accountant friend, Dana, did it for Zach—while she was dating Finnegan."

"What?"

"She rubbed it in by carrying Zach's child."

The other shoe dropped, and Sienna's head spun. Had Dana been sleeping with both Mr. Ford and Gavard?

Better yet, had Gavard used Dana for the express purpose of stealing money from his wife? Why would Gavard need it?

"Zach and I were unable to have children," Celestia explained. "You can imagine how broken I was when I found out Dana was pregnant."

"I thought that was Mr. Ford's child." Sienna

figured that everything would be clear after Dana delivered the child.

"Could be, but Finnegan told me that he had a fight with Dana, and she stopped talking to him for a couple months. However, Zach was all too happy to *talk* to her."

"I don't...I mean, this is confusing," Sienna said.

"Nothing confusing about it. I'm divorcing Zach, and I want my money back."

"So you took money from the GOOP funds?"

"Only what's mine."

"Did Dana do it for you?" Sienna had to know.

"Funny how it works. Dana stole from me for Zach, and I hired her to steal the same amount back from GOOP for me."

"Why didn't you take money from Mr. Gavard himself?"

Celestia laughed. "He's broke, dear. He's been raiding the GOOP coffers too."

"What?" Sienna couldn't believe it. Could it be possible that the top leadership of the company had been draining it dry? How could they possibly get away with such a thing?

Celestia laughed. "If you didn't already know, Zach and I have lavish lifestyles."

"What about Mr. Ford? How is he involved?" Sienna asked.

"Finnegan was my fall guy. Only he died on me." Celestia sighed.

"Is that the truth?"

"Might as well tell you. Killjoy has prepared a feast for the sharks she has been feeding." Celestia smiled, but there was pain in her smile, as though she was reluctant to kill Sienna. "I wish I didn't have to, you know? You're a good worker, and I wanted you to work for me. I really did. However, we're beyond that now."

Celestia's face turned into a hardened look. "If you don't want to die, then open the safe."

"My hands are tied."

Celestia looked at Killjoy again. "Untie her."

Sienna felt the restraints around her wrists loosen. Then they were gone. She flexed her arms and massaged her wrists. She tried not to look overjoyed that her bracelet was still there. Ironic.

Indeed God had used it all for good.

Let my rescuers find me soon, Lord Jesus.

"Did you pay off Agent Kimball?" Sienna asked.

"Who?"

Sienna heard the answer like a giant bell tolling. It meant that Kimball messed up on her own.

"You know what the Bible says about money,"

Sienna stood there. "I Timothy 6:10 says, 'For the love of money is the root of all evil: which while some coveted after, they have erred from the faith, and pierced themselves through with many sorrows.' You love money, sorrow comes."

"Sorrow?" Celestia laughed. "It came a long time ago."

"Did you kill Rocco and Arun?" Sienna blurted.

"Stop asking questions and open the safe."

Someone prodded Sienna on the back, pushing her forward. Probably Killjoy.

"How do I know you won't kill me anyway?" Sienna asked as she walked to the safe. She knelt down. Killjoy was standing next to her. The hench-woman's tall boots went all the way to her knees. They were polished black, but her shoelaces were red.

"We're just going to throw you overboard. The sharks will feed on you. Good for the ecosystem, good for us. End of story."

"Then at least tell me what you and Mr. Ford did to pull it off. I need to know for my own conscience."

"Open the safe and I'll tell you."

"How about you tell me as I open the safe.

There's something inside that needs a password too."

"So you do know about this safe." Celestia snapped her fingers. "Then I will humor you with stories you wouldn't believe."

"Like what?"

"Some of us have been skimming off the top of GOOP for years in ways you don't expect," Celestia said. "Technically, if you use a pen from work to write your own non-work things, you're stealing."

"Except in Mr. Ford's case it's billions of pens?"

"Mr. Ford? Surely you jest." Celestia laughed again. "Finnegan was freaked out about helping me get even against Zach. He was afraid the company would go under. I had to tell him it had already gone under."

Poor Mr. Ford. "Perhaps the situation was so bleak that his heart gave out on Friday."

Celestia shrugged. "He was a good friend, but we must move on. Open the safe."

Sienna did as she was told. She remembered the code that Mr. Ford had told her. The safe opened like a charm.

"The hardest part was for Joy to get the safe from Tybee Island to the Bahamas." Celestia laughed. "Give me the laptop."

Sienna handed it to her.

Celestia opened it. "Log in. You know the password."

Once again, Sienna did as she was told.

Quietly, the laptop booted up.

"Looks like it might be running out of battery," Sienna said. "Who knows how long Mr. Ford had that laptop in the safe. I need to check the safe for a power cord."

"Go ahead." Celestia motioned for Killjoy to look at their find.

As both of them pored over the laptop, Sienna opened various drawers inside the safe. She spotted a phone. And realized what Mr. Ford had been up to. She turned on the phone and left it on. She saw the icon coming alive, showing that the laptop was now tethered to the phone and transmitting something somewhere.

To whom?

Sienna didn't know at this point.

Even though Helen Hu told him to wait for her, Earl did not. His quick and cryptic call to Leland Yang-Joule at Binary Systems opened up all sorts of doors at the NSA. Once Leland located the bracelet that Sienna was hopefully still wearing, the CIA got involved because the yacht was on international waters and one of GOOP's investors, Mr. Lee of Canada by way of Hong Kong, was wanted for his involvement in an investigation that Earl wasn't privy to.

One thing led to another, and Earl Young ended up reuniting with an old friend, Dario de la Cruz, who flew him to a vessel at sea, from which the Mendenhall Security team launched inflatable boats that took them across the water toward the Blue Sea Diamond superyacht. In the dark of night, they shot grappling tools into the air, and climbed aboard the yacht.

It was utter chaos, and half the time Earl wasn't sure where he was because he wasn't used to the night vision goggles. He found himself running down a hallway, ducking to avoid getting shot at, and then hiding behind anything that looked like steel. Thankfully, his Special Forces training from years ago kicked in, and he soon picked up speed and kept in step with the Mendenhall team.

Then he heard calls for help.

"Sienna?" It sounded like someone else, but she could be nearby.

He radioed the team leader as he ran toward the voices. Somewhere he could hear the thwack-

thwack of chopper blades. Either more Mendenhall Security team members were dropping in, or someone was leaving.

The voices got louder and louder. Behind him came six or seven former military guys. The locked door posed no barrier to them as they broke it down.

Two women inside. Both had their wrists tied up.

"Sienna!" Earl shouted her name.

"Earl?" Her voice sounded shocked. "Am I dreaming?"

"No, you're not. I'm here." He sliced the ties around her wrists.

"Thank God!" Sienna exclaimed. "If you'd come tomorrow in the morning, we would not have been here."

"Why?"

"Shark food."

"Not on my watch." Earl grabbed her hand as they ran out, surrounded by armed Mendenhall Security personnel.

"Genevieve!" Sienna tried to look back.

"We got her," someone said. "She's with us. We're going to get you out of here."

"It's Celestia," Sienna told Earl.

"What?"

"Killjoy works for Celestia," Sienna said. "She had me open Mr. Ford's safe. His laptop is in the—"

A bolt of lightning brightened the sky above the yacht, revealing the entire top deck. Mendenhall Security surrounded them, battling Killjoy's people, pushing them away from Earl, as he led the two women toward the chopper waiting for them at the other end of the top deck.

It started to rain. The superyacht rocked a little on the waves. Through his night vision goggles, Earl thought he saw a swelling ocean. Great.

"Hurry! We need to get to the chopper before the storm comes." Earl pressed forward.

Before he knew it, Earl found himself flat on the deck, the wind knocked out of him. A knee was on his chest, a weapon pointed at his head. He looked up into the eyes of evil.

Killjoy?

He could hear women screaming around him. Sienna?

Suddenly, the knee lifted off of him. The pressure on his chest lightened. Earl caught his breath. Through his night vision goggles, he saw Sienna and Genevieve struggling with his attacker, pulling her away from him. They rolled on the tipping deck.

A shot rang out.

"Sienna!" Earl yelled, rushing toward the brawl.

Genevieve slumped back and went motionless.

Sienna screamed.

Earl took the opportunity to aim his Glock. "Get behind me, Sienna!"

He wasn't the only one shooting back at the armed Killjoy.

One of the Mendenhall Security personnel came over to Earl. "Get out of here!"

"Let's go home," Earl ran toward the chopper with Sienna in his arms.

CHAPTER NINETEEN

Seven months after they buried Genevieve in Atlanta next to Mr. Ford's grave, the sun shone bright over Tybee Island, but the December weather was cool enough that Sienna didn't break a sweat driving the moving van to her new beach house. Earl was in the passenger seat, the muscle man who had gone with her to Chattanooga to haul the remaining boxes from Uncle Tabbebo's house.

A promise was a promise. So those three dozen boxes of war memories and children's toys from Uncle Tabbebo's family and also Mom's would remain in Sienna's basement—probably forever— while her uncle and Mom moved into the

Savannah Senior Living Resort for the rest of their lives.

Sienna backed the van into the driveway and opened the garage door remotely. She got out of the van as Earl was still on the phone with Helen Hu, who seemed to have plenty of work for him to do at Hu Knows, Inc. So far, since they had returned home from the Bahamas, Earl had been gone a lot. That old adage, "absence makes the heart grow fonder," applied to them.

Earl had told her that every time he was away, he couldn't wait to get home to see her again. Sienna had her own things to deal with, so she kept busy enough such that she didn't miss Earl too much.

Mariana Kimball lost her FBI badge over the mishandling of three GOOP employees. Whistle-blowers Dana and Sienna nearly lost their lives.

Thankfully, Dana had entered WITSEC, and not a moment too soon. Sienna didn't have to because the storm was over and the criminals caught. She was told that Dana might come out of WITSEC soon, although she might opt not to, for the sake of her child.

Sienna wondered what sort of deal Dana had made with the FBI to allow her to be in WITSEC instead of in jail. After all, she was very much involved in the embezzlement. If not for her, neither Celestia nor Gavard could have funneled that much money out of the GOOP bank accounts.

Sadly, coworker Arun lay buried in an Atlanta cemetery. His child would have to grow up without him. His wife had filed a lawsuit against the FBI and the federal government. She remained in the country as her child was born here, and was thus an American citizen.

On trial, Celestia Gavard faced years in jail for embezzlement, hiring Killjoy the henchwoman— and falsely imprisoning Sienna aboard a yacht. Her attorneys claimed that she only tried to salvage what was left of her scheme when her partner-in-crime and mastermind of it all, Mr. Ford, passed away suddenly. The twenty-one-billion-dollar company funds Celestia tried to abscond were reparation for having to put up with an adulterous husband who had slept with both his personal assistant, Noreen, and the company accountant, Dana, and impregnating the latter.

Regardless, her schemes had backfired because Mr. Ford had another failsafe in place. When Sienna activated the phone inside the safe, it transmitted everything Celestia typed on the laptop to Mr. Ford's lawyer in Atlanta, who then turned the evidence over to the state and federal prosecutors.

In other words, Celestia didn't stand a chance in court. And Mr. Ford had the last laugh over his half-brother Zachary and his sister-in-law Celestia.

As for Joy "Killjoy" Burditt, there was nothing much to say except that she had lived by the sword and died by the sword. It was too bad that she had not been alive to testify against Celestia or explain how she had found the FBI safe house. However, killing a federal agent would have brought a severe penalty that would have been probably worse than a quick death onboard Celestia's superyacht.

The other vehicle door opened and slammed shut. Earl stretched and then walked toward Sienna, who was walking toward her mailbox. "That was a long drive."

"Yeah, six hours." Sienna shuffled her mail. Mostly advertisements. "Good thing you came with me and drove for three hours."

"Glad to help." Earl walked with her.

Seven months after they had met, they stopped pretending as their relationship continued beyond the GOOP whistleblowing operation that the FBI had wrapped up. Zachary Gavard gave his full cooperation in exchange for a shorter sentence, even though everyone knew that GOOP, as they knew it, was over. Even Noreen quit her job there.

Earl had tried to persuade Sienna to apply for

the administrative assistant position at Hu Knows, but the more Sienna learned about the private investigation firm, the less she wanted to work there. She didn't need the pressure and stress.

After much prayer and introspection, Sienna decided that she did not want an office romance with Earl. She'd rather meet him after work hours so that they could have different things to talk about outside of work.

She joined Earl's church, Riverside Chapel in Savannah, some fifteen minutes from her new house—which she had purchased when Mr. Gavard gave her a generous severance package. At church, she met Priyanka Patel-Jacobs, doctor-in-residence at the Savannah Senior Living Resort, which Sienna had hoped would take Mom and Uncle Tabbebo.

It just so happened that they were looking for an office manager. Sensing it was an opportunity from God for a change of scenery and pace, Sienna applied. Lo and behold, her extensive corporate experience landed her the job. GOOP was good for her career, after all. Both Priyanka and the SSLR Director, who was also her cousin, Dr. Roger Patel, were pleased with how Sienna cut office waste, cleaned up the office management system, and added efficiency to their daily operations. The ministry became a blessing to many, and the waiting list shortened as new wings opened up with more rooms.

Since she moved to the area, Sienna had lunches with Earl every day, sometimes at the SSLR dining room or garden and sometimes in town in Savannah, where the Hu Knows headquarters was.

Four months after Sienna started working at SSLR, a resident passed away at SSLR and another left to live with her grandchildren out of state. Sienna was thrilled to get the call that room was finally available for both her mom and uncle. Earl helped her move them from Chattanooga to Tybee Island, where Mom's health improved as she spent time outdoors in the garden, greenhouse, and by the Atlantic Ocean. She even made new friends while playing Bingo, her dementia notwithstanding.

Uncle Tabbebo himself had taken a fancy for one of the pretty widows at the residence, and decided it was time to sell his house in Chattanooga. Thus began the process of hauling his war memories, medals, and old books, plus Mom's own boxes of family stories to Sienna's basement.

Earl opened the back door of the moving van. He reached for the cooler. "Want some water?"

"Yes, please." Sienna took stock of what they

had stuffed into the van. There was an old lamp, suitcases, moving boxes. "How did we get all those things into the van, just the two of us?"

"We chatted and listened to music and the news, so maybe it didn't feel like work," Earl said.

"We also took our time." Sienna recalled that it had taken them two days to load up the van. They stayed in separate hotel rooms nearby, but between the two of them, they had cleaned up Uncle Tabbebo's house before the listing agent showed up to take photographs of the house for their real estate advertisements.

Earl nodded, handing her a bottled water. "Shall we take a little break before we carry the boxes into the basement?"

Sienna nodded. "I need to check on Wyclef, and then we can unload the van. So glad Cade could come over and feed him the last two days."

Earl nodded. "He's good with pets, though he only has dogs of his own."

Sienna entered the garage and unlocked the door leading to the kitchen. She disarmed the alarm.

"Wyclef!" She called out. Then she turned to Earl. "Can you believe it? No welcome party."

Wyclef came over, his fur all ruffled like he had been napping.

"What? Did you sleep all day while we were gone?" Sienna picked him up in her arms. "I thought you're our guard cat."

Earl laughed. He checked the house and the three rooms, and then returned.

"All okay?" Sienna asked, even as she knew that her alarm hadn't gone off. Still, when Earl went into protective mode, the best thing was to let him be.

"Yeah. Looks fine." Sienna let Wyclef down. She brushed off cat hair stuck to her goose down jacket.

Earl looked warm in just a down vest over a few layers of flannel. He was walking around the kitchen, checking windows and the door leading to the porch.

Sienna unlocked the back door for Earl, and they stepped outside onto a covered porch over-looking the ocean.

The air was fresh and clean, but Sienna felt cold. She zipped up her jacket all the way to her neck, and wished she had worn a long coat to cover her legs. Her pair of jeans wasn't thick enough to ward off the cold winter air coming up from the Atlantic Ocean beyond the yard and dunes.

"I can't believe Sabine found you this little gem." Earl drew a deep breath.

"God provides. She looked for such a house for months," Sienna said. "I really like her and I'd recommend her to anyone who wants to buy or sell a house."

Earl nodded. "Both Sabine and her husband, Ming, are great Christians. They speak the truth and never let you down."

"I remember Sabine giving me a reality check when I asked for a small oceanfront beach house. She said that many years ago, she sold another beach house like this one to her sister-in-law. However, she said it's rare. Most of the time, people either keep them or mow them down to build a bigger house, and then sell those for way more than I can afford. Then she found this house in foreclosure. Good for me."

"Three bedrooms are enough to raise a family in," Earl said.

"You mean the resale value?" Sienna took another sip of water.

"That too."

Sienna looked out at the ocean. "What a view."

When Earl didn't reply, Sienna turned around—

And gasped.

Earl was on one knee. In his hand was a small red velvet box.

"What's happening?" Sienna could hardly breathe. She hadn't expected this.

"Are you surprised?" Earl popped open the red box.

"I'm shocked." Sienna couldn't recall any of their conversations lately pertaining to marriage per se. However, they had talked about raising children. A lot. "Why today?"

"If I wait for the right moment, that may never come. Today is just as right a moment as any other time."

Sienna gave him a look. "Is there another reason?"

Earl cleared his throat. "Helen is sending me out of town for an undercover operation through Christmas and New Year's. I don't want to carry this ring with me and wonder whether you've found someone else."

"There's no one else," Sienna said quietly.

"SSLR residents with eligible grand-nephews and grandsons would beg to differ." Earl sounded serious. "They show up at Christmas in droves to see their grandmas and grandpas."

Sienna smiled. Earl had been jealous before, and she didn't want to bring up the times when he wouldn't let Deshon talk too much in the vehicle on their drive from Atlanta to Macon.

"Sienna, I've been in love with you since the second week we met," Earl began. "I can't stop thinking about you when we're not together, and when I'm with you, I don't want to leave."

"Someone told me that I should trust God for him," Sienna said. "You can trust God for me too."

"I trust God for you, Sienna. I've prayed about this for several weeks. The more I pray, the more certain I am that God has brought you to share my life with me—my joy and sorrow, my happiness and pain, and everything in between."

Sienna sniffled. She felt the same way about Earl as well.

"I'm happy to just be with you. I'll help you with your mom and uncle. I'll carry out the trash every night. I'll vacuum and cook and clean—on second thought, for the last part, I'll hire a maid for you." He chuckled.

Sienna giggled. "Are you being silly?"

"Seriously, I can't bear to be without you." Earl paused. "Sienna Bethany Halstead, will you marry me? There is no one else I'd rather spend my life with than you."

Sienna was so happy that tears streamed down her cheeks. In spite of the cold breeze, she felt warm inside, her heart full of peace, love, joy, and certainty that God had brought them together, as Earl had said earlier.

"Yes, I'll marry you, Earl Ambrose Young, and make you my one and only husband in my entire life. There is no one else I'd rather be with. May God guide us according to His perfect will."

After Earl placed the diamond ring on her finger, he lifted her up in the air and twirled her around on the porch, laughing with her and hugging her. Then he put her back down on her feet.

His kiss was soft and gentle.

"Kiss me like this for the rest of my life," Sienna whispered.

"Yes, dear." He repeated his sweet caress.

Above them, the sea birds called. Beyond the grass and sand, the ocean waves roared and cheered.

CHAPTER TWENTY

Sienna and Earl wanted to marry as soon as possible, so they picked a date five months after Earl's proposal, but Sienna's mother passed away in her sleep two days before the wedding.

Sienna's grief caused them to postpone their big day, and it turned out to be a good thing, as Sienna and Earl spent more time getting to know each other as they met for lunch and dinner daily.

Gentleman Earl didn't rush Sienna. He stood by her side, waiting. He told her to take all the time she needed to grieve for her mother, but Sienna knew he was probably also praying that she would get through the hardest part of her grief journey soon so that they could be married.

Her father came down to Savannah from Dahlonega to comfort her, and it was then that Sienna realized how much older her father looked. In fact, his second wife had passed away a couple of years before. Sienna was afraid that she would lose Dad too—even though she knew that their lives were in God's hand.

One year after she buried her mother, Sienna was ready to start a new life with Earl.

So here they were.

Sienna didn't feel harried this Saturday morning in May, two years after she had met Earl. It was interesting to her that seven months into their relationship, Earl had known for sure that he wanted to marry her. Their engagement had been a happy occasion, with Sienna growing to love Earl more and more in the months following it. Sienna knew there was no one else she'd rather marry than Earl Ambrose Young, even if their wedding was delayed.

Sienna had always been careful about her spending, and she was shocked to find out how much a wedding costs. Adding that to the expense of paying for her mother and uncle at Savannah Senior Living Resort, she could barely afford the reception. It was bittersweet that Mom passed away before the wedding, but Sienna would rather have had her mother alive with her than to have a lavish wedding.

Everyone had been kind to them, saving them an enormous amount of money. Donovan Moss gave Sienna a discount on the garden venue for the wedding at the oceanfront Moss Tybee Resort on Tybee Island. And it came with a wedding planner. He also gave them a discount at his island resort in the Bahamas, where they would spend their week-long honeymoon. Helen Hu prepaid for their business-class plane tickets. The rest of Earl's colleagues came together to gift them their first married month's house payment.

"Such practical gifts," Uncle Tabbebo had said. "My kind of people."

There he was down the hotel hallway, walking toward her now, wearing a charcoal suit with a white gardenia boutonniere. Gardenia was Mom's favorite flower.

Sienna held back her tears. If she let them flow, she'd never make it to her own wedding ceremony.

"The guests are waiting," Uncle Tabbebo said. "The garden is lovely, not as cool as I expected even though it's only nine o'clock."

"Thank you for the weather report."

"Your mother would've loved to be here, but

let's be happy for her that she is now pain-free and frolicking in the green meadows of heaven."

"Are there meadows in heaven?" Sienna asked.

"I don't know, but whatever God has prepared for us will be beyond anything we can see on earth." Uncle Tabbebo patted Sienna's hand.

"I'm so glad you shared Christ with Mom before dementia took her."

Uncle Tabbebo nodded. "I've tried to witness to her for many decades, as you know. Somehow after all her adventures, she had returned to me for one last chance to tell her about what Jesus had done for her on the cross."

A door opened nearby, and Dad appeared.

"I'm praying for your dad," Uncle Tabbebo whispered in her ear.

"Thank you." Sienna smiled.

"Let's go." Dad lifted his elbow on one side of her.

Uncle Tabbebo also lifted his elbow for her.

After all that Uncle Tabbebo had done for Mom and herself, Sienna couldn't imagine not letting him walk her down the aisle. However, in recent years, she had reconciled with her estranged father, and traditionally, the father of the bride would do the honors.

So here they both were.

As for a bridesmaid, Sienna had none. She wondered how Dana was doing in WITSEC, whether she had a safe childbirth. Someday, Dana might appear again in Sienna's life. Or not.

Sienna prayed for Celestia and Gavard. God could still forgive their souls, if only they would repent of their sins and humble themselves before God. Celestia had written back from prison, rejecting both ideals, and adding that she and Gavard were still corresponding.

Sienna didn't have the heart to remind Celestia that Gavard would serve less time than she would, although his carte blanche had enabled Celestia to hire and pay off rogue FBI agents and assailants. After all, Gavard had divorced Celestia and testified against her. No doubt when he was released, he would move on with his life and leave Celestia to languish in prison. Or so, Sienna suspected.

"Let the past go," Uncle Tabbebo said, as if reading her mind.

Sienna was stunned. Was she holding on to the past? Quietly, she prayed for her friend Dana, surrendering her to God. Ironically, if not for Dana, Sienna would not have become a whistleblower and called Helen Hu for help, and therefore she would not have met Earl.

Down the hallway, violin and harp music grew louder through the stained-glass doors leading to the outside garden.

Dad cleared his throat, and he slowed down. "Sienna, I'm so sorry for all that I have done to you and to your mother. I am sorry."

Sienna blinked, trying not to get tears on her mascara. "I forgive you, Dad."

He squeezed her hand in his. "Thank you."

"Now you two guys be strong, okay? Exercise, eat right, stay healthy, all that." Sienna smiled. "I want you both to be around when Earl and I have kids. We need babysitters."

Uncle Tabbebo moved his other arm back and forth. "I'm starting right now. I'll join the gym next week."

Sienna laughed as the door opened to the sky and a garden filled with gardenia and roses. Their hundred-plus guests smiled as the music rose to a crescendo with the "Wedding March."

At the end of the petal-strewn aisle, Earl and his two best men—Deshon and Cade—stood like statues frozen in time. Earl's eyes widened and he looked positively stunned.

Under a canopy of puffy clouds and sea birds going about their day, Sienna walked forward in the morning breeze, an occasional gust pushing her mid-length bridal veil back and forth around her shoulders and bare arms.

When Dad and Uncle Tabbebo handed Sienna to Earl, she could hear her future husband say, "Wow."

The ceremony went as rehearsed, with Pastor Diego Flores reading Bible passages about holy matrimony and love and future children.

It was all too real now, and in spite of everything having been planned, Sienna's hands started to shake. She had never been this nervous before in her entire life. It seemed now that being an administrative assistant was easier than going through a wedding ceremony.

"I now pronounce you husband and wife," Pastor Flores concluded.

What?

Sienna blinked. They had sailed through the wedding vows and ring exchange. She looked down at her ring finger. Yes, the wedding band was there.

She prayed she had not botched up the wedding vows because it went so fast that it was all over. Perhaps Earl had been right. They should not have decided on such a short ceremony. They wanted it to be short and sweet so that they could run off to their honeymoon as soon as possible.

But first, the reception.

E arl relived every minute of the wedding ceremony, remembering the ring exchange with great excitement. Sienna had been nervous, but so was he. When Pastor Flores told him he could kiss his bride, Earl made sure to kiss Sienna long enough to calm her nerves.

Well, they were both still nervous when they walked down the aisle to cheers and hollers. It was only when they had a quick moment of privacy before they headed to the reception in the Moss Tybee ballroom that Earl and Sienna were able to catch their breath.

He caught her hand and led her down a quiet hallway. Gently, he planted a kiss on her forehead.

"We're finally married," he whispered in her ear.

Sienna smiled. "We've known each other all of two years."

"We have the rest of our lives to get to know each other more, starting tonight." He caressed her cheek with his fingers and then lifted her chin to his—

A ping stopped him.

He turned toward the echoing sound. Down the hallway, Helen Hu was swiping her pinging phone as she stood still. She looked worried. Then again, Helen always looked worried.

"Something is wrong," Sienna said.

"How did you figure that?" Earl asked, not letting Sienna go.

"I can read people's faces—and Helen's face says something is up or someone is down."

"You sure?" Earl leaned toward his bride.

"Go check."

"No."

"Then I will." Sienna tried to wiggle out of Earl's embrace.

"No. It's our wedding day, Sienna. We're officially not working for two weeks, remember?"

"Give me two minutes. Please?" Sienna pleaded.

Earl sighed. "Why is Helen more important than I am?"

"She's not." Sienna held his hand and dragged him down the hallway. "Come on. This is our happy day. I don't want to see anyone upset or worried. Let's take care of it and send her on her way."

"Okay. Whatever." Earl realized he had just

learned the first lesson of his married life. "See? I'm listening to you."

"Thank you. I listen to you too."

They rounded the corner. In the rotunda leading to the ballroom, Helen was talking animatedly with Hugo, Deshon, and Cade.

"What's going on?" Earl asked as he approached them.

"Stay out of this," Helen said. "Sienna, take him to the reception. They're probably waiting for you two to cut the cake."

"Is everything okay?" Sienna asked.

Helen didn't say a word.

Deshon and Cade weren't about to override their boss, Earl figured.

"Hostage situation in Miami," Hugo said. "Pilar Santiago is in the middle of it. She might be injured."

"Oh no." Sienna leaned against Earl's arm. "Does Ming know?"

Earl was impressed that Sienna remembered how they came to know Pilar. It was via his friend Ming Wei, another private investigator in Savannah with his own company, Savannah River Investigations. At one point in time, Earl almost became a partner in SRI, before Helen offered him a promotion.

"Ming is in Miami now, but he needs some help," Helen said. "I don't want to be the bringer of bad news to my sister, so this is serious."

With three kids and one more on the way, Ming's wife, Sabine, would probably be very worried. Earl wondered whether there would come a time when his life was in danger, and Sienna was left having to handle their kids and thinking about his well-being.

"We need to pray," Sienna said.

Helen nodded. "Miami SWAT and CNT are on it, but Pilar and Ming were working on a surveillance operation before they got caught in the crossfire. Ming escaped, but Pilar did not."

"I'm packed and ready to go," Cade said. "Send me."

"Send me too," Hugo said. "Ming's my friend."

"He's my friend too," Earl said.

"You're going to Port Lucaya," Helen said to Earl. "Hugo is going back to Brussels. I'm taking this one. Cade can come with me."

"You?" Hugo asked. "If you go to Miami, we all want to go with you."

"Isn't that wonderful?" Helen said. "But if something happens to me, you need to run Hu Knows, so we can't both be in the same operation at the same time."

Hugo nodded. "Who's going to run the Savannah office? Earl is on vacation for two weeks."

Sienna turned to Earl. "We're only in the Bahamas for one week. We'll be home the following week."

"Right. We'll be here in case you need us."

Helen pointed to Deshon with her red fingernails. "You up to the task of running our Savannah office for one week all by yourself?"

"Yes, ma'am." Deshon nodded. "Plus I get to stay free at Earl's house."

"And feed my cat," Sienna said.

"Our cat," Earl corrected her. "Wyclef Halstead-Young."

"Yes, our cat." Sienna wrapped her arms around Earl's waist.

He placed his arm around her shoulders. "Let's pray and ask God to keep us all safe."

"Go ahead." Helen closed her eyes.

"Thank you, Father God, for bringing us here today for a blessed wedding day," Earl prayed. "Please keep Ming and Pilar safe right now in Miami. Protect Helen and Cade as they fly to Miami to rescue them, and Hugo as he returns to Brussels."

"And keep Earl and Sienna safe on their honeymoon," Hugo prayed. "Lord, bring all of us back together again safely. In Jesus' Name, I pray. Amen."

Everyone said *amen*.

"Sorry to spoil your day," Helen said to Earl and Sienna. "But Cade and I can't stay for cake. When we return, we can have dinner at my house."

"On Santorini?" Earl's jaw dropped.

Helen nodded. "Ruben is a great cook. We would love to have everyone over. Maybe we can have a company retreat for our families."

Earl nudged Sienna. "See the perks of working for Hu Knows?"

Sienna smiled.

Earl didn't want to nag her any further for choosing to work at SSLR instead of at Hu Knows with him. At the end of the day, it was a good thing for them to separate their office work from their home life.

From the corner of his eye, Earl saw someone waving to them. It was Sienna's Uncle Tabbebo, motioning the bride and groom to get on with the program.

"Ah, our guests are waiting," Sienna said.

"Keep us posted." Earl held Sienna's hand. "We'll pray for you from the Bahamas. If we need to be there, we can fly to Miami in an hour."

"I'm sure we don't need you," Helen said. "Go

enjoy your honeymoon. There will be plenty of hard work waiting for you when you get back."

"Thank you. We'll see you in a week." Earl led Sienna away to the reception hall.

They stepped into the ballroom to the cheers and applause of their wedding guests and well-wishers.

Putting aside work and the trouble in Miami for a moment, Earl wrapped his arms around Sienna's waist and drew her to his chest. The music started playing around them, a waltz of some sort that Earl wasn't familiar with. Instead of dancing, Earl brushed his cheek against Sienna's and held her in his arms. Then he kissed the edge of her lips, coaxing a smile out of her.

"I thank God for you," he whispered in Sienna's ear, and held her for a long time.

Dear Reader:

Thank you for reading *Never a Traitor*, book 1 in my Defender Sweethearts collection of Christian romantic suspense. While *Never a Traitor* is about Earl protecting Sienna in the Caribbean, the next novel, *Never a Hostage*, takes us to

Miami where Helen and Cade meet up with Ming to rescue Pilar. Or is Pilar rescuing them instead?

Never a Hostage (Defender Sweethearts Book 2): JanThompson.com/hostage

Many of the supporting cast of *Never a Traitor* have their own books in the Protector Sweethearts and other series set in the same story world.

- Helen Hu and Reuben Costa are in Once a Thief (Protector Sweethearts Book 1)
- Jake Kessler is in Once a Hero (Protector Sweethearts Book 2)
- Corazon Garcia-Moss and Donovan Moss are in *Twice a Fighter* (Protector Sweethearts Book 4)
- Donovan Moss is also in Smile for Me (Vacation Sweethearts Book 1)
- Cade Sumter and Pilar Santiago are in *Never a Hostage* (Defender Sweethearts Book 2)
- Pilar Santiago is also in Look for Me (Vacation Sweethearts Book 4)

- Deshon Kernaghan is in *Never a Champion* (Defender Sweethearts Book 6)
- Cayson Yang and Stella Evans are in Zero Sum (Binary Hackers Book 1)
- Kelvin Gallagher is in Zero Day (Binary Hackers Book 2)
- Dario de la Cruz is in *Zero Base* (Binary Hackers Book 3)
- Priyanka Patel-Jacobs is in Kiss You Now (Savannah Sweethearts Book 7)

Some of these books are published and some are coming soon. Sign up for my newsletter to receive book news when the next book is coming.

Subscribe to Jan's Book News:
JanThompson.com/newsletter

A free romance ebook set in the same story world:
JanThompson.com/time-free

While waiting for *Never a Hostage* to be published, how about reading the sister series, Protector Sweethearts, if you haven't already? In *Once a Thief*, Private investigator Helen Hu must team up with art thief Reuben

Costa to rescue her mother, who vanished while trying to make amends for stealing some bejeweled eggs that could lead to the lost Amber Room.

Once a Thief (Protector Sweethearts Book 1)
JanThompson.com/thief

Continue reading for a sneak peek of *Once a Thief*.

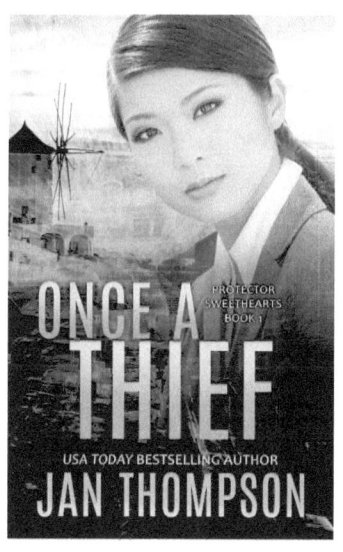

A plunge away from the Aegean Sea, the town of Oia hugged the Santorini cliffs of the caldera, a haunting reminder of a volcanic past ever present in Helen Hu's mind as she parked the ATV and set off on foot down the pedestrian walkway.

Her company-issued iPhone told her where to go through the mishmash of cliffside buildings and tourist-packed lanes meandering around painted fences, containers of brightly colored flowers, and tiny blue hotel pools. The pastel-colored buildings looked like interlocking Lego blocks glued to the side of the rocky mountain.

Every now and then, Helen spotted blue domes, mushroom caps reaching toward the afternoon Mediterranean sky, portending bright days ahead.

Not!

The signal grew stronger. Helen spotted her mom in the crowd.

Mom was way ahead but slowing down now as she pretended to weave in and out of souvenir shops, stopping to touch a postcard or two, as if to leave fingerprints in case something happened to her.

What, Mom? What?

Swept into a wave of tourists and their multilingual tour guides, Helen quickened her steps across the uneven lanes sandwiched among shops and restaurants, villas and guest houses, private properties and potted bougainvilleas—all the while trying to keep an eye on Mom.

Mom had a distinct walk. Helen could spot her a mile away, always in one of her many identical pairs of five-inch-heeled jacquard boots. Those boots added inches to the diminutive woman and brought Mom to about Helen's height.

And those boots slowed Mom down enough for Helen to catch up to her in the crowded lanes and paths.

Helen suspected Mom wasn't here on Santorini on a quick weekend getaway—without her signature luggage when she had gotten off the ferry from Athens an hour ago.

So what is she here for?

Mom had made no attempt to hide. Her fuchsia blouse was bold and matched some of the flowering plants contrasting the surrounding white and blue architecture.

Every now and then, Mom would glance back, as if searching for something, looking for someone.

Meeting someone?

Helen looked away, just in case Mom spotted her. Even at sixty-eight, Mom's eyesight was way better than Helen's. And she had often said that she could identify either one of her daughters from miles away.

Helen wasn't about to test that now.

Not after all the trouble she had taken to get here. The notification had arrived while she had been in the middle of hunting down a fugitive passing through Frankfurt.

While Helen's Hu Knows, Inc., private investigative firm specialized in recovering lost art and missing persons, the company had grown and expanded into tracking down fugitives—since the day they had successfully helped the FBI apprehend an international terrorist who had abducted Helen's mom and sister.

Her sister had gone on to marry and have kids.

But Mom.

Mom had retreated into her own little world after that episode.

Sometimes Helen wished that Mom would be more forthcoming with her. Since Dad had passed away so many years ago, Mom had tried to carry on with her life in fits and starts. As the years had gone by, she had withdrawn more and more into the recesses of her own thoughts and memories.

And now? Was this a part of Mom's multiyear introspection?

Helen felt a burden to care for her mom. At thirty-four years old and with no prospects of marrying and having children, Helen felt that she had more time than her sister to take care of Mom. In fact, Mom was already living with her back in Savannah.

Helen wouldn't mind if Mom lived with her the rest of her life. She wanted Mom to know that her daughters really wanted the best for her and that it was time for Mom to be transparent.

Yeah, right.

Helen pushed through the crowd toward Mom, as more people swarmed around Helen, down the steps and narrow walkways, looking for balconies to park themselves and set up video cameras and smartphones for their sunset viewing.

Sunset would be in two hours.

When Dad had been alive, they had come here often during summer vacations, only to see the sunset and to cruise on the Aegean Sea. Dad had been quite a yachting enthusiast. Helen and her sister, Sabine, hadn't taken to the water as much as Dad and Mom had. Sometimes their parents would take their own vacation.

The two of them would end up in Santorini—also known as Thira—or they'd sail to Crete, across the water, where they would stay in a villa owned by an old family friend.

Helen stopped.

Her iPhone signal showed that Mom had been inside that souvenir shop for over a minute.

Helen held her breath and ran, her black boots pounding the cobblestones beneath, the summer sun above her baking her baseball cap and shoulders.

Before Helen reached the souvenir shop, she heard the noise of a motor overhead. A drone in the sky hovered.

Someone taking photos?

She heard a popping sound.

Then another.

And another.

Pop! Pop! Pop!

Someone screamed, and the crowd went berserk.

The racket of screams and shrieks turned into a stampede as the tourists scattered like ants in the narrow lanes, any way they could to get out of the bottleneck, pushing and shoving Helen and everyone else in their paths.

Children and babies crying, people jumping over the low fences into hotel pools, people falling down as they were mowed over by shoes and knees and a mob gone wild.

Helen elbowed her way toward a low iron gate, thinking she could climb over it to safety.

Before she could get there, something whizzed past her ear—

And she went flying to the ground, sacked like a quarterback, sandwiched between the dirty cobblestone-and-cement lane and someone on top of her.

All around her were hot wafts of stinky shoes from the maddening crowd, the odor of sweat and fear—

And a sudden, distinct, clean smell of fresh soap.

"Get off me!" Helen's elbows and torso twisted this way and that to get the man off her back. She almost hit him with her iPhone, which was still in her grip.

He barely moved.

"Get off me!" she repeated, thinking he couldn't hear her in the concert of loud and chaotic footfalls.

"Shhh. It's still above." His voice was calm. Accented.

And definitely male.

The summer sun continued to beat down on them. The man's weight pushed Helen's backpack against her spine, probably crushing her iPad and magazine inside.

Police sirens blared in the distance, and the drone sounds eased away.

"We have to get out of here," the man said.

"Then get off me!"

As soon as the man eased off her, Helen wiggled out from underneath him as quickly as she could, her right hand reaching into her waistline pistol pouch—

"Helen!"

She heard the familiar sharp tone above the roar of the crowd.

She looked up, squinting in the shifting sunlight and shadows. She realized then that her sunglasses had been knocked off her face. "Mom?"

Mom tapped the ground with her boots. "What in the world are you doing here?"

Instead of giving Helen a hand, Mom leaned toward the man who had rolled off Helen.

He was trying to get up. He clutched his chest. "What sharp objects do you have in that backpack?"

"You okay?" Mom asked.

Helen scooted back against the gate to prevent herself from getting kicked by the rushing crowd.

"I think I'm okay." She brushed dirt and grime off her clothes.

"Not you. I meant him." Mom picked some grass off the man's hair. "I see you two have met—or shall I say, made contact."

Helen's eyes widened. "Please tell me you're not dating a man half your—"

"No, no. He's not my type. In fact, I think he's more your type."

"Mom!" Helen rose to her feet too quickly. The world swirled around her.

But strong arms caught her before she fell.

She smelled a whiff of clean, fresh soap again.

Male cologne.

Continue reading the rest of the story in ebook or paperback format:

Once a Thief (Protector Sweethearts Book 1)
JanThompson.com/oncethief

Protector Sweethearts
JanThompson.com/protector

Subscribe to Jan Thompson's mailing list:
JanThompson.com/newsletter

ACKNOWLEDGMENTS

Many thanks to my Georgia Press publishing team for keeping up with my writing schedule.

Thank you to editor Lesley Ann McDaniel for copyediting and proofreading this novel.

A special thank you to my loyal readers who have been with me from the beginning. You've waited patiently for me to write my books, and you never let up over the years. May God bless you!

I am grateful to God for my husband and son for their support and encouragement. I also thank God for my parents and my three brothers for my happy and memorable childhood. I'll always remember my beloved mother and my late father for having instilled in me the love of reading and writing from a very early age. I miss my father here on earth, but I will see him again in heaven someday.

Most of all, I am eternally thankful to my Lord and Savior, Jesus Christ, who died on the cross to save me from my sins and rose again from the grave to give me eternal life. Without Him, I can write nothing (John 15:5).

Joyfully in Jesus,
Jan Thompson
John 3:16

HYMN: ALAS AND DID MY SAVIOR BLEED

Alas, and did my Savior bleed?
And did my Sovereign die?
Would He devote that sacred head
For such a worm as I?

Chorus:
At the cross, at the cross where
I first saw the light,
And the burden of my heart rolled
    away,
It was there by faith I received my
    sight,
And now I am happy all the day!

Was it for sins that I had done

He groaned upon the tree?
Amazing pity! grace unknown!
And love beyond degree!

Well might the sun in darkness
    hide,
And shut His glories in,
When Christ, the mighty
    Maker, died
For man, His creature's sin.

Thus might I hide my blushing face
While His dear cross appears.
Dissolve my heart in thankfulness,
And melt mine eyes to tears.

But drops of grief can ne'er repay
The debt of love I owe;
Here, Lord, I give myself away,
'Tis all that I can do.

The lyrics for this "Alas and Did My Savior Bleed" hymn penned by Isaac Watts in 1707, with additional chorus by Ralph E. Hudson are in the public domain.

BOOKS BY JAN THOMPSON

Contemporary Christian City, Coastal, and Beach Romance

Seaside Chapel (7 Books)
JanThompson.com/seaside
Savannah Sweethearts (12 Books)
JanThompson.com/savannah
Vacation Sweethearts (8 Books)
JanThompson.com/vacation
Midtown Christmas (4 Books)
JanThompson.com/christmas

Christian Romantic Suspense and Near-Future
Technothrillers

Protector Sweethearts (6 Books)
JanThompson.com/protector
Defender Sweethearts (6 Books)
JanThompson.com/defender
Binary Hackers (4 Books)
JanThompson.com/binary

Subscribe to Jan Thompson's mailing list:
JanThompson.com/newsletter

SEASIDE CHAPEL

Welcome to *USA Today* bestselling author Jan Thompson's Seaside Chapel Christian beach romance series. These novels are set on real-life St. Simon's Island, Georgia—a beach town where history is all around and the future is a moment away—and the neighboring fictitious Seaside Island, where the rich and famous live.

Savor the small-town atmosphere and the warm southern beaches of St. Simon's Island and the idyllic Golden Isles along the Atlantic Ocean. Enjoy the music of the orchestra and hymns of the church, and hang out with our Christian friends who attend Seaside Chapel, a little church by the sea known for its beach weddings and fair share of love and life.

As these Christians grow in their knowledge and understanding of God, they are tested in their spiritual maturity, their love lives, and their relationships with others. Share their heartaches and healing, and cheer them on as they celebrate faith, family, and friends.

JanThompson.com/seaside

- Book 0 (Prequel): *His Surprise Proposal*
- Book 1: *His Longing Heart*
- Book 2: *His Wake-Up Call*
- Book 3: *His Morning Kiss*
- Book 4: *His Quiet Serenade*
- Book 5: *His Waiting Love*
- Book 6: *His Beach Retreat*

SAVANNAH SWEETHEARTS

Welcome to the new south! From *USA Today* bestselling author Jan Thompson come these clean and wholesome, sweet and inspirational Christian romances set on the romantic beaches of Tybee Island and in the coastal town of Savannah, Georgia. Meet a group of multiracial and multiethnic churchgoing Christians who love the Lord, work hard in their careers, and seek God's will for their love lives. Against a backdrop of ocean, sand, and sun, these inspirational romances showcase aspects of the human need for God and for one another. Have some tea, settle in a comfortable reading chair, and enjoy these sweet celebrations of faith, hope, and love in Jesus Christ.

JanThompson.com/savannah

- Book 1: *Ask You Later* (Artist Romance)
- Book 2: *Know You More* (Multiracial Romance)
- Book 3: *Tell You Soon* (Asian-American Romance with Suspense)
- Book 4: *Draw You Near* (International Romance)
- Book 5: *Cherish You So* (Wheelchair Billionaire Romance)
- Book 6: *Walk You There* (Old-Meets-New Tour Guide Romance)
- Book 7: *Love You Always* (Romance with Suspense)
- Book 8: *Kiss You Now* (Multiracial Romance)
- Book 9: *Find You Again* (Multiracial Romance)
- Book 10: *Wish You Joy* (Christmas-Themed Romance)
- Book 11: *Call You Home* (Deaf Chef Romance)
- Book 12: *Let You Go* (Asian-American Romance with Suspense)

Read *Ask You Later* (Book 1) for free:
JanThompson.com/ask-free

VACATION SWEETHEARTS

Travel with our friends from Savannah, Georgia, to the coast and to the mountains. Cheer them on as they celebrate the immeasurable grace and undeserved mercy of God through Jesus Christ.

The Vacation Sweethearts novels are a spin-off of Jan's Savannah Sweethearts series, and fans will recognize familiar faces from Riverside Chapel, a church in the coastal city of Savannah, Georgia. In fact, we might even visit the beach town of Tybee Island from time to time to visit old friends and beloved families...

JanThompson.com/vacation

- Book 0 (Prequel): *Time for Me*
- Book 1: *Smile for Me* (International Romance)
- Book 2: *Reach for Me* (Romance with Suspense)
- Book 3: *Wait for Me* (Romance with Suspense)
- Book 4: *Look for Me* (Romance with Suspense)
- Book 5: *Pray for Me* (International Romance)
- Book 6: *Care for Me* (Small Mountain Town Romance)
- Book 7: *Cheer for Me* (International Romance)

Read *Time for Me* (Prequel) for free:
JanThompson.com/time-free

MIDTOWN CHRISTMAS

Big city romance, small town feel. Four Christian couples minister at Midtown Chapel in metro Atlanta, and Midtown Village, the community of tiny homes for needy families. From November to January every year, this place turns into a Christmas Village for a small-town feel right there in the metropolis of Atlanta, Georgia.

- Book 1: *Let Me Hold You* (Levi Theroux and Maggie Jacobs from *Pray for Me*)
- Book 2: *Let Me Want You* (Erika Song from *Look for Me* and Hiroki Yamada from *Walk You There*)

- Book 3: *Let Me Need You* (Forsythia McDevitt from *Call You Home* and Owen Grayson from *Find You Again*)
- Book 4: *Let Me Love You* (Leila Patel from *Find You Again*)

PROTECTOR SWEETHEARTS

Private investigator Helen Hu and her associates specialize in searching for missing persons and hunting for lost treasures. Join them in their adventure suspense around the world in *USA Today* bestselling author Jan Thompson's Protector Sweethearts, a series of Christian Romantic Suspense with a side of mystery.

Protector Sweethearts is a spin-off of Savannah Sweethearts and Vacation Sweethearts.

JanThompson.com/protector

- Book 1: *Once a Thief*

- Book 2: *Once a Hero*
- Book 3: *Once a Spy*
- Book 4: *Twice a Fighter*
- Book 5: *Twice a Convict*
- Book 6: *Twice a Soldier*

DEFENDER SWEETHEARTS

Defender Sweethearts is a sister series to the Protector Sweethearts Christian romantic suspense collection. While the heroes in Protector Sweethearts search for lost treasures and lost people, the Defender Sweethearts novels focus on protecting the helpless and hopeless. The main characters in Defender Sweethearts come from the supporting cast in Protector Sweethearts.

JanThompson.com/defender

- Book 1: *Never a Traitor*

- Book 2: *Never a Hostage*
- Book 3: *Never a Fugitive*
- Book 4: *Always a Maverick*
- Book 5: *Always a Champion*
- Book 6: *Always a Guardian*

BINARY HACKERS

Like more suspense with your Christian romance? Like to read suspense thrillers? If you're looking for clean near-future romantic suspense without compromising the Christian faith, these books are for you.

From *USA Today* bestselling author Jan Thompson come these inspirational near-future cyberthrillers combining technothriller and romance, starting with Binary Hackers that feature computer specialists living at the edge of cyber-space, where they have to juggle being law-abiding truth-telling Christians while carrying out their assignments by any and all means possible.

The Binary Hackers series is set in the same story world as Jan's other books, and characters from the other series may make cameo appearances in this series and vice versa.

JanThompson.com/binary

- Book 1: *Zero Sum*
- Book 2: *Zero Day*
- Book 3: *Zero Base*
- Book 4: *Zero Trust*

ABOUT JAN THOMPSON

USA Today bestselling author Jan Thompson writes clean and wholesome contemporary Christian romance with elements of women's fiction, Christian romantic suspense with an air of mystery, and inspirational international thrillers with threads of sweet Christian romance. Jan's books are for readers who love inspiring stories of faith, hope, and love in Jesus Christ.

Raised on a tropical island in the eastern hemisphere, Jan now lives and writes in the western hemisphere. Her international background gives her a unique multicultural and multiracial perspective to her novels and books. The island has never left her, and she reminisces about beach life in her beach romance novels.

When Jan is not busy writing small-town stories, she writes big-city romantic suspense and international technothrillers, a nod to her previous career in computer science. She weaves technology with human interests, reflecting the current and future digital world. And romance. There's always romance.

Beyond the printed page, Jan is a wife, mother, family scribe, avid reader, occasional artist, erstwhile pianist, and chief of staff to the family cat.

Find out more about Jan Thompson:
JanThompson.com

Subscribe to Jan's book news mailing list:
JanThompson.com/newsletter

For God so loved the world,
that He gave His only begotten Son,
that whosoever believeth in Him should not perish,
but have everlasting life.

—John 3:16